Praise for the Lords of Vice novels

Dusk with a Dangerous Duke

"Hawkins's writing is effortless, free-flowing and very eloquent." —*Under the Covers Book Blog*

"*Dusk with a Dangerous Duke* was tantalizing and sexy." —*My Book Musings*

"A satisfying and good read." —*Rakes, Rogues and Romance*

"I could not put *Dusk with a Dangerous Duke* down." —*Romance Novel News*

All Afternoon with a Scandalous Marquess

"I love this series and its decadent heroes." —*Romance Dish*

"A good, solid choice for historical fans." —*Night Owl Romance*

"One of the best in the series." —*The Good, The Bad and The Unread*

"If you love historical romances, then this is a must-read." —*Romancing the Book*

Sunrise with a Notorious Lord

"Simply spectacular from front to back!" —*Fresh Fiction*

"A clever and passionate story with a plot twist or two that grabs your attention and holds on right up to the wonderful ending." —*Romance Junkies*

"These Lords of Vice only get more and more interesting as the series goes on. They make sexy and sinful feel like satin sheets you want to roll around in until you're sated and exhausted."
—*The Good, The Bad and The Unread*

"Smart, sexy, and fun." —*Romance Novel News*

"Regency fans will enjoy the bold heroine and rakish hero." —*Publishers Weekly*

"Alexandra Hawkins writes some of the best stories set in the era!" —*Huntress Reviews*

"Charming, fun, and sexy." —*RT Book Reviews*

"Hawkins is pure magic that captivates her readers from cover to cover." —*Romantic Crush Junkies Reviews*

"There is never a dull moment when the Lords of Vice get together!" —*Romance Dish*

"*Sunrise with a Notorious Lord* is a fun and lively story."
—*Romance Reviews Today*

"This book starts on a fast pace and never slows down."
—*Reading Reviewer*

"Her Lords of Vice definitely live up to their names."
—*Limecello*

After Dark with a Scoundrel

"I absolutely loved *After Dark with a Scoundrel*. It is an amazing read and I could not put it down . . . I can't wait for the other Lords of Vice." —*Night Owl Romance*

"Those sexy Lords of Vice return as another member is caught in a maze of love and danger. Hawkins's talents for perfectly merging gothic elements into a sexually charged romance are showcased along with the marvelous cast of characters taking readers on a thrill ride." —*Romantic Times BOOKreviews* (4 stars)

"A 'must-read'. . . *After Dark with a Scoundrel* is a fast-paced Regency historical romance with a new and exciting surprise just about every time you turn a page . . . as stunning as it is riveting. This story has it all . . . scorching." —*Romance Junkies*

"The sparks between Regan and Dare are beautifully written, so that you can almost feel them coming off the pages." —*Book Reading Gals*

"4½ stars. The intensity between Regan and Dare sizzles on the pages." —*Romance Dish*

"Ms. Hawkins knows just how to pull the best from her characters to make you care for them, love them, get irritated with them, and all those other delicious emotions we romance readers need in our books."

—*The Good, The Bad and The Unread* (A+)

"Perfect explosion of emotional fireworks blasted off the pages and set the rest of the tone for the book."

—*Romantic Crush Junkies* (4.5 quills)

"Poignant, sweetly romantic, and sexy as can be."

—*Reader to Reader*

Till Dawn with the Devil

"*Till Dawn with the Devil*'s romance is first-rate with unusual characters and an underlying mystery that will intrigue readers."—Robin Lee, *Romance Reviews Today*

"A terrific second book in this series. I had it read in a day and then bemoaned the fact it was over."

—*The Good, The Bad and The Unread* (A+)

"You will devour every sexy and intriguing morsel of this divine read." —*Romantic Crush Junkies* (4 stars)

"Hawkins cements her reputation for bringing compelling, unique, and lush romances to fans eager for fresh storytelling." —*Romantic Times BOOKreviews* (4 stars)

"Delightful and enjoyed every delicious minute of the book." —*Single Titles* (5 stars)

"You will devour every sexy and intriguing morsel of this divine read." —*Romantic Crush Junkies* (4½ quills)

"An absolutely tantalizing read!"
—*Huntress Reviews* (5 stars)

"Her characters are vibrant, sincere, and will surely steal your heart." —*Romance Dish* (4½ stars)

"Alexandra Hawkins is making a splash in historical romance and fans of the genre who haven't read the Lords of Vice series should sit up and take notice."
—*The Season*

"Promises an intoxicating journey, and delivers with an exciting series of twists and turns that leave the reader disoriented and begging for more." —*Fresh Fiction*

"Alexandra Hawkins did a splendid job of weaving believable characters, palpable attraction, and a soundly satisfying plot line that will leave you *panting* for more!" —*Not Another Romance Blog* (5 red roses)

All Night with a Rogue

"Sizzling, smart, and sophisticated."
—*New York Times* bestselling author Gaelen Foley

"Wickedly sensual and entertaining! Alexandra Hawkins is an exceptional talent."
—*New York Times* bestselling author Lorraine Heath

Also by
ALEXANDRA HAWKINS

Dusk with a Dangerous Duke

All Afternoon with a Scandalous Marquess

Sunrise with a Notorious Lord

After Dark with a Scoundrel

Till Dawn with the Devil

All Night with a Rogue

Twilight with the Infamous Earl

Alexandra Hawkins

TWILIGHT WITH THE INFAMOUS EARL

For information address St. Martin's Press, 175 Fifth Avenue, New York, NY 10010.

ISBN: 978-1-250-00139-9

Printed in the United States of America

St. Martin's Paperbacks edition / December 2013

St. Martin's Paperbacks are published by St. Martin's Press, 175 Fifth Avenue, New York, NY 10010.

10 9 8 7 6 5 4 3 2 1

This book is dedicated to the fans of the series. Your love and boundless enthusiasm for the Lords of Vice have meant the world to me. It's been an amazing journey!

Vice is perhaps a desire to learn everything.

—Honoré de Balzac

Chapter One

April 1, 1826

"Am I boring you, Frost?"

Vincent Henry Bishop, the Earl of Chillingsworth, who many knew simply as Frost, allowed his hand to slide appreciatively over the contour of his current bed companion's naked waist and hips. Widowed two years ago—if there was any validity to the rumors—the thirty-five-year-old Lady Gittens was on the hunt for a new husband.

If true, the dear lady had deplorable taste in men if she considered him a candidate for marriage.

"Did I seem bored five minutes ago?" His fingers separated as Frost cupped one of the fleshy cheeks of her buttocks.

He and the delectable widow had spent the better part of three hours in the lady's bed. His companion was enthusiastic and inventive. The cooling sweat on his flesh and his pounding heart were proof that he had been fully engaged in their love play.

Maryann was reclining on her side with her buttocks teasingly close to his still-rigid cock. Frost sensed her smile.

"Not at all. Five minutes ago I managed to command all of your attention."

He brushed aside her dark blond hair that was sticking to her damp flesh. "When I'm with you, I need all of my wits," he murmured, kissing her on the bare shoulder.

"Then why have you have checked your watch three times in the past hour?"

Although he had tried to be discreet, her plaintive tone implied it was a considerable offense. "And that is my sin?"

Women. They fretted over the oddest things.

"The hour is growing late, my sweet. As much as I enjoy our encounters, I have other obligations."

"Another woman?"

Frost sighed. He and Maryann had been lovers for three weeks, and she was already displaying signs of possessiveness. Even though he had made it clear that she was not his only lover, the lovely widow was pressing him to set aside his other women. She thought she could dictate the terms of their little arrangement, and for a time he had been willing to indulge her whims.

Unfortunately, spoiled creatures tended to become tedious over time.

"Yes." She stiffened in his casual embrace. He hid his smile in her hair. "My sister. I've been commanded to make an appearance this evening."

Maryann made a soft scoffing sound. "No one commands you, my lord."

He playfully swatted her on the buttock. She cried out in surprise.

"It is good of you to notice." There was a slight warning in his tone, but his companion was oblivious. "However, I make a point of listening to Regan. She has a nasty temper when provoked."

Maryann shifted in his embrace until her back was pressed against the soft mattress. She gazed up at him with limpid blue eyes. "Your sister is not the only one who gets cross when she doesn't get her way."

Frost gazed down at her body. She was a beautiful woman. White, unblemished skin that still held a ruddy blush from their lovemaking, full breasts with erect nipples, and generous hips that bore the marks of his hands and teeth. The thatch of hair between her legs glistened with the evidence of their lust. "You should have no grievances with me. You've had your way for half the afternoon, wench," he said teasingly.

"Only because it pleased you to do so," she said with a pout.

"And that is why we have gotten along famously." He lightly ruffled the hair between her legs and kissed her on the lips. "You understand me all too well."

With some regret, he began to rise. "I should go."

Something akin to panic flashed across Maryann's flushed features. She reached for his wrist to halt his escape. "There is no rush. It is early still, my love. Tarry awhile longer."

The temptress parted her thighs as she guided his hand to her womanly folds. His cock stirred with approval as his fingers tested the proof of her desire.

Frost hesitated. Sensing her victory, she arched her hips, the action allowing his fingers to deepen their penetration.

The three hours they had spent tangled in the sheets had passed quickly. If he had not promised his sister that he would join her and their friends for dinner, he would have stayed until his body was fully sated.

Frost grimaced. "I have no time for this."

He withdrew from Maryann.

Her eyes snapped open with frustration. "How can you possibly stop now?" she demanded.

"With much difficulty and regret." He covered her hand with his and gently peeled her fingers from his cock. "Be reasonable, my sweet. I do not want to start something that will take us hours to finish."

"Then give me an hour more," she pleaded, crawling after him when he stood. "Just one. I promise you will be grateful you granted me this boon."

Without warning, Maryann dropped to her knees and took him into her mouth. She suckled the head of his arousal with enough pressure to make him groan with pleasure and discomfort. The lady possessed an exquisite mouth.

His fingers brushed her shoulders. "Maryann." He drawled her name in a manner that was an equal balance of praise and curse.

It only took him a second to come to a decision.

"Stop."

Stunned by his order, Maryann released him and lifted her bewildered gaze to meet his. Frost pounced. Hauling her to her feet, he spun her around and bent her over until her hand found purchase on the mattress.

She laughed with delight. "Yes, please, my lord."

Frost was not seeking her permission. He used his foot her widen her stance as his hand curled around the length of his hard flesh. "Is this what you want?"

His vigorous thrust filled her and she gasped at the swift invasion.

"Yes. Hard and fast. Let's not waste a minute of the hour!"

Seizing her roughly by the hips, Frost set a pace that would have made a seasoned prostitute at a brothel wince. However, Maryann moaned in pleasure as he buried himself into her sheath over and over.

Frost suspected he would be late for Regan's gathering, but his sister would forgive him. His gaze admired the curve of Maryann's spine as he reminded her who was in control of their relationship.

He intended to pleasure her for the hour he had promised, and then he would walk out of her life without a single regret.

Chapter Two

"Lord Chillingsworth," Lord and Lady Pashley's butler announced as Frost entered the dining room three and a half hours after he had first joined Lady Gittens in her bed.

"Good evening, all," Frost said to the twelve people sitting at the long rectangular table. Lord Pashley, or Dare, who also happened to be his brother-in-law, was seated at the farthest end. All six gentlemen were as familiar to him as his own reflection in the mirror. His friendships with Dare, Hunter, Saint, Sin, Reign, and Vane were formed when they were still boys. As for the ladies, with the exception of Regan, who was his sister, claiming any kind of familiarity with Grace, Catherine, Juliana, Sophia, and Isabel real or just fanciful wishing on his part would likely end with his jaw being broken, since the ladies were happily married.

Over the past six years, his dearest friends had fallen in love and married. As often was the case, the demise of their little band of merry bachelors had begun with Sin.

The Marquess of Sinclair or Sin, as he was often called, was so besotted with Juliana, no one except Frost had foreseen the consequences of what his friend had started. One by one, his friends had sacrificed their freedom for the marriage bed.

He was surrounded by couples, Frost noted with silent amusement, and he, the lone bachelor of their little group. "Ah, I see it is just family this evening. Good, I am famished."

He bent down to kiss his sister's cheek.

"You are late," Regan said, tilting her cheek to accept her brother's kiss, which was part affection and part apology for his tardiness. "If you were so famished, you should have arrived before the first course was served."

"My apologies, brat. Something came up unexpectedly."

The six gentlemen seated at the table smirked and chuckled at his response. There was a good reason why the *ton* referred to the seven of them as the Lords of Vice. His friends could hazard a guess on how he had spent his afternoon.

Frost had little doubt the ladies had guessed as well.

After all, his little sister had been practically raised by him and his friends. Too often, she had glimpsed compromising situations that had made her old beyond her years.

Regan gave him a knowing glance. "Indeed." She grasped his left ear before he could escape, pulling his head down so she could kiss him on the cheek. "You have been missed, brother mine."

Frost briefly shut his eyes as he savored his sister's caress, and then he pulled away. Regan was the only woman who had a claim on his heart. She was proof that he was not the coldhearted bastard he had often been accused of being by angry mistresses and half the *ton*.

He acknowledged his brother-in-law with a nod. Dare had been his friend long before the gent had set his sights on Frost's little sister. Believing Regan deserved someone better than a Lord of Vice for a husband, Frost had tried to discourage the relationship. He had even sent his sister away to Miss Swann's Academy for Young Ladies in the hope that time and distance would extinguish Regan's affection for the handsome scoundrel. Alas, his efforts to keep the young lovers apart had failed, but he was not disappointed with the results. Not only had he gained a brother, but Dare had proven to be an excellent husband and father.

"My apologies for disrupting your conversation," he prompted his host so Regan could not question him further on why he was late for their dinner party. "What did I interrupt?"

Dare was not fooled by his friend's apology or feigned interest. He likely deduced that anything Frost had to say was best discussed away from the ladies. Shrugging, the man said, "We were discussing your nephew's new game of repeating every word he hears."

"And how is the lad?" Frost leaned back in the chair while the footman placed fine china and silver cutlery on the table in front of him. Now eighteen months old, Bishop Wells Mordare held the lesser title of Viscount Wrenne. He was a beautiful boy with his father's good looks, his mother's mouth, and his uncle's charm. It would be a potent combination as young Bishop grew older.

Dare shook his head and sighed. "Bishop overheard your sister and the housekeeper discussing a slight mishap in the kitchen." At Frost's raised eyebrow, he explained further. "It was nothing. Some crockery was knocked over and one of the maids cut her hand as she picked up the shards."

"How tragic," he drawled, earning him an amused look from Saint's wife, Catherine.

A bowl of what looked like milk soup was served. Perhaps goat's milk? With a delicate shudder, he signaled the footman to remove it. Regan displayed her displeasure with a slight pout. Thankfully, she resisted the urge to scold him. Boiled mackerel with a fennel and mint sauce swiftly replaced the unwanted soup.

Dare took a sip of his wine. "Well, a few hours later, Lady Netherley called on Regan. Of course, she insisted on seeing Bishop when he awoke from his nap."

"Naturally," Frost said, laying his linen napkin across his lap. "The lad has been charming ladies since he was pulled from his mother's womb."

Vane paled at the casual mention of the birthing process. His wife, Isabel, was in the seventh month of her pregnancy, and this was their first child. It mattered little to his friend that many of the ladies seated at the table had given birth to healthy infants.

Vane fretted over his lady. He blamed himself for Isabel's delicate condition, and rightly so. Unfortunately for his sweet-natured wife, she would have an overbearing husband on her hands until she delivered Vanewright's heir.

"Bishop adores Lady Netherley. She doesn't understand most of his chatter, but she enjoys her brief visits with him." Dare winked at Vane, who happened to be the elderly marchioness's son. "She is anxious for her new grandchild to be born."

Isabel placed her hand on her rounded belly. "She isn't the only one," she said, sounding tired.

Dare and Regan shared a rueful smile. "When Regan settled Bishop on Lady Netherley's lap, he said rather clearly, *'Mama bwoke cocks.'*"

Sin burst out laughing. Dare, Reign, Saint, Vane, and Hunter joined him, while the wives fought back smiles. Regan's eyes watered as she tried not to laugh. It was not the first time his friends had heard the tale, but the humor of it had not grown stale in the retelling.

"I was dreadfully embarrassed," Regan confessed, using her napkin to dab at the moisture in her eyes as she laughed. "Especially when Lady Netherley asked Bishop to repeat his words because her ears were weary that day."

Frost smirked at his sister. "I'll wager you whisked our boy out of the drawing room before he could utter a sound."

Regan closed her eyes and groaned. "And you would be correct, dear brother." She gave Saint and

Catherine an impish grin. "See what you have to look forward to?"

The implication was obvious.

The Marchioness of Sainthill was carrying Saint's child.

The announcement came as a slight surprise to Frost. Although it was not common knowledge, Catherine's upbringing was vastly different from those of the other ladies at the table. There was also a little history between him and Catherine, but their tryst was so brief it was barely worth mentioning. On one occasion, Saint had privately admitted that Catherine was concerned she might be incapable of having children when she had not conceived a child during the first year of their marriage. Thankfully, their good news proved that her worries were unfounded.

"I say, congratulations are in order," Frost said, raising his glass of wine to the couple. "A toast to Catherine and the health of her unborn child. May the son possess the temperament of his sire!"

Saint grinned, looking ridiculously pleased with himself. "Frost, only you could make a toast sound like a bloody curse."

"To Catherine and Saint," his companions echoed.

The next two hours passed by in a leisurely albeit noisy fashion. Instead of the gentlemen adjourning to Dare's library for brandy and port, they had joined the ladies in the drawing room. It wasn't long before Bishop's nurse appeared at the threshold with the little charmer rubbing the sleep from his eyes. Regan gathered her son in her arms and strode over to Dare.

His friend's gaze lit up with joy and love as Bishop reached out for his father.

It was a good thing he hadn't quietly murdered Dare when the gent slipped Regan out of the house one evening and married her without Frost's consent. Regan's happiness meant more to him than his pride, though he would never admit it.

Soon his nephew was joined by Sin and Juliana's son and Reign and Sophia's little girl. High childish shrieks of delight and dismay were heard over the din of the adult conversations. To add a little civility, Juliana offered to play one of her recently published musical compositions on the pianoforte.

If the marchioness hoped that music might calm the little beasts, her efforts were in vain.

Frost brought his fist to his mouth to conceal his laugher as the lady's son zigzagged around the room with a small replica of a tall ship clutched in his hands. Even more entertaining were Sin's futile attempts to catch the lad.

"Did you ever think you'd ever witness the day that Sin was bested by a child?" Saint asked as he approached Frost. In his hands, he had two glasses of brandy. Thankfully, he was willing to share.

"Never." Frost accepted the glass and took a sip. "Though to be honest, Sin's expertise lay in chasing skirts rather than little boys. Do you know what you are getting into?"

Frost was referring to the announcement of Catherine's pregnancy and Saint's impending fatherhood. The brilliant smile on his friend's face was more eloquent than words.

"Does anyone?" Saint shrugged. "If I can persuade Catherine, I'd like to fill the nursery."

Frost chuckled, shaking his head in disbelief. There was a time when he would have wagered that no lady could have claimed the marquess's heart. "You might want to pace yourself, gent."

The sound of breaking porcelain and a sharp cry of indignant outrage spared Saint from replying. Sin had finally caught his son, and in the process had knocked over a large vase. Juliana had abandoned the pianoforte and was attempting to soothe her crying son. Sin stepped aside, relieved his wife was willing to take charge of the situation.

Perhaps in sympathy for their upset friend, Bishop and Lily began to cry. Sophia rushed to her daughter's side while Dare dealt with his son.

"Is this a drawing room or a nursery?" Frost wondered aloud, but no one was paying attention to him.

As the children sobbed, and the adults tried to calm them, Frost watched, realizing that he was the one who did not fit the quaint family gathering. Somewhere along the way, his friends had moved on without him when they had married and started their families.

He was part of their lives, but no longer one of them.

Frost finished his brandy as he mulled over his unpleasant revelations about himself and his friends. There were other things to consider, as well, like the future of Nox.

"Are you just going to stand there gathering wool?"

Dare demanded, his frustration penetrating Frost's dark musings. "A little assistance would be welcome."

Frost smirked. "I think not, dear brother. This is when I will quietly take my leave. Please, carry on with your evening without me."

He turned away from his family and friends. Alone. Just the way he preferred his life.

Chapter Three

In a small country graveyard, Emily stared solemnly at the headstone that marked the final resting place of her beloved older sister.

Lucille Charlotte Cavell
Born February 2, 1801
Died August 19, 1821

Family and friends had called her Lucy, and everyone had loved her. Betrothed to Lord Leventhorpe, she should have been happily planning her autumn wedding.

Instead she had perished by her own hand.

Five years had passed since that tragic night when Emily had discovered her sister alarmingly pale and bleeding on the floor of her bedchamber. Lucy had been barely conscious when Emily screamed for her father as she gathered her dying sister into her arms.

"Hold on. Father will know what to do!" she had assured her sister, her slender fingers unable to halt the blood spilling from the ragged wounds on Lucy's wrists.

"Love," her sister murmured almost sleepily. "It ruins what it should treasure."

"Stop talking. Conserve your strength," Emily had told her.

She shouted for her father again, but the muscles in her throat had constricted with growing horror that her sister was too far gone to be saved by anyone. Her voice cracked as she sobbed in frustration.

"Emily?"

Lucy had sounded surprised to see her.

"Yes." Emily glanced about the room wondering if there was something she could use to bind Lucy's wounds. She was reluctant to leave her side, but no one had heard her cries for assistance.

Her sister's glassy green gaze seemed unfocused, and her increasing lethargy frightened Emily.

"I have to go find Father. You need a surgeon."

"No," Lucy replied with unexpected strength. It quickly faded on her exhale. "Just listen. I need you to listen."

Emily bowed her head over her sister. Her last words were a confession of her sins. It was a burden she did not wish to carry forth in death. So Lucy had passed her darkest secrets to her.

"Tell no one," she had begged. At Emily's blank stare, she demanded, "Swear."

"I swear" had been her numb reply.

Her mother's high-pitched scream snapped Emily out of her stupor.

"What have you done?"

Turning away from her daughters, she called for her husband and the servants. Lucy had been pulled from Emily's arms and placed on the bed.

Emily sat in a pool of her sister's blood as they had tried to save her. She did not have the voice to tell her mother and father that Lucy had no desire to be saved. She had wanted to die.

And she had succeeded.

"You have to let her go," her mother said gently, coming closer until she was standing behind her. "Lucy loved you. She would insist that you be happy."

"I am happy, Mother," Emily replied somberly, her gaze still focused on the headstone.

"You might have your father fooled, but a mother knows what's in her daughter's heart." Her mother placed her arm around Emily's waist.

She thought about Lucy's last words. "Truly? Did you know what was in Lucy's heart when she sliced her wrists open with Father's blade?"

It was rather spiteful of her to ask a question to which she already knew the answer. Her mother had not been privy to her eldest daughter's secrets. A soft choking sound of shock and the loss of her mother's comforting embrace was the least she deserved.

"This melancholy is about London, is it not?" Her mother's voice had hardened at the not-so-subtle reminder that Lucy was beyond their reach because her family had failed her. "You are looking for a reason not to join us."

"Of course not, Mother." She leaned down and placed the bouquet of flowers she was holding next to the headstone. "I look forward to joining the family in London."

Emily offered her mother a slight smile.

Her mother still looked unconvinced. "You have avoided—"

She resisted, rolling her eyes. "This old argument. First, I was too young to join you, and other years, I wished to spend my time with friends."

"In the country," her mother lamented.

"It is not a sin to have good friends." Emily teased to lighten the mood. "Besides, I will see them in London this year. This should please you."

She had won the battle without much effort, and she was suspicious. "And you intend to join us in the festivities. Balls, the theater, the museums—"

"All, and more," Emily assured her.

"Oh." The lines in her forehead eased. "Well, that's wonderful. Your father will be delighted to see us." Her mother clapped her hands together. "Just wait until we go shopping. You will be amazed by the assortment and quality."

Emily did not interrupt her mother as she spoke of her favorite shops. She had not lied. After all, she was looking forward to traveling to London. Her mother and father had high hopes for her this season, and she planned to enjoy all the amusements the town had to offer.

Nevertheless, there was one small task she intended to keep from her family.

While she was in London, Emily intended to find the gentleman who had ruined her sister and use everything at her disposal to return the favor.

Chapter Four

There were very few things that could ruin Frost's mood.

Unfortunately, the lady who had written the note he had clutched in his fist was at the top of his list. To add to his annoyance, she had not bothered making an appearance at the meeting she had requested.

It was so typical of her.

Frost strode across the lobby of the hotel and stepped out onto the street. He raised his hand, blinking against the glare of the afternoon sun. Belatedly, he recalled that he had ordered his coachman to return for him in one hour.

Softly cursing under his breath, he debated on whether he should return to the hotel. There was always a chance his companion was late for their meeting.

He swiftly discarded the notion.

The lady was playing unpleasant games with him. If she required his assistance, she could bloody well seek him out. He had no intention of lurking around the lobby in the hope of catching sight of her.

Too agitated to sit, Frost crossed the street with no specific destination in mind. The exercise would do him good. It would clear his head and work off his temper. He was not going to let her ruin his afternoon. The days when he was at the mercy of her whims were long gone, and she knew it.

Old habits were difficult to shed.

The hotel was respectable, but it wasn't situated in the most fashionable section of town. However, this time of day, pedestrians and hawkers selling wares filled the walkways, and there was a steady stream of horses, wagons, and coaches on the streets. As long as he avoided the narrow mews and alleys, no one would challenge him. And if some unlucky fellow was foolish enough to cross him—well, then, he was willing to accommodate him.

With his walking stick in hand, he kept his pace leisurely as he noted the passing carriages. It was probably too much to hope that his coachman would make a timely appearance. A light breeze teased his hair, reminding him that he preferred to be outdoors rather than closed up in a stuffy room.

Perhaps he should view the missed appointment as a blessing in disguise. There were more pleasurable ways to enjoy the afternoon.

As he passed what barely counted as a street, a woman's cry of pain caused him to turn his head. Halfway down the street, a fight was brewing. Spectators were already forming a circle around what seemed to be a disagreement between several women and a man. He was too far away to distinguish their words, but the woman in blue was angry.

Not your concern, gent.

Fights broke out daily on the London streets. Jealous rivals engaging in fisticuffs, merchants bumping chests over what was perceived as a competitive advantage, whores shouting after customers who had cheated them out of a proper payment—Frost had witnessed it all.

He did not need to involve himself in their affairs.

Then the man grabbed one of the women. As he attempted to drag her away from the crowd, the other female attacked him with her unopened parasol. The man knocked his attacker aside as he wrestled with the first woman.

Frost despised bullies.

He headed for the trio, slightly annoyed that no one could bring themselves to help these women. As he drew closer, he quickly noted the differences between the two women. The female being dragged off was the younger of the pair. She was wearing a dress that was too large and should have been tossed in the rag bin years ago. The man's rough handling had torn one of the sleeves, and there were dirt smudges on her skirt. The second female did not belong in this rough borough—although she did not appear to be worried about getting her hands dirty. Her white gloves, the lace and workmanship of her blue dress and bonnet, and her prim educated voice as she berated the beefy bruiser all marked her as a lady of quality.

She was also a redhead, Frost observed, as several crisp curls had slipped free during her struggles.

He had a fondness for redheads.

"Let her go," the woman said, her chilly cultured tones warming Frost's heart. "If you leave now, with luck on your side, you might avoid being dragged before the magistrate."

"If anyone is going to jail, it's you," the man jeered, unimpressed with the woman's threat. "This wench is my property. You have no right, stealing her from me."

"Me?" The redhead's slender body vibrated with outrage. "That child is no man's property, you worm! Furthermore—"

"Perhaps I might be of service?" Frost smoothly interjected, his polite query causing the two women and man to stop and gape at him. On closer inspection, he had to reevaluate his opinion of the female in the dirty dress. She was more child than woman. If she was older than sixteen, he would eat his boots. If she had worn a bonnet, she had lost it while struggling with her captor. Her dirty brown hair was unbound and her thin, pinched face spoke eloquently of the poverty she endured. Her brown eyes were bloodshot from crying, and there was a wild, desperate look in them that angered him. The girl was frightened.

"None of this is your business," the man was saying to him. "Nor is it yours, witch!"

The redhead did not take kindly to being called a witch. "Oh, so I have the look of a witch, do I?" she asked in mocking tones. "What gives me away? My red hair or my green eyes?"

She took an intimidating step toward him, and the man had the good sense to retreat. "I'll share a little secret with you. If I was a witch, I would turn you into a fat rat and then give your skull a solid thumping with my broom!"

Several spectators chuckled, which only enraged the man.

His face reddened as he mopped the sweat on his brow with his free hand. "See here, you—"

"Before you finish your threat, I suggest you release the girl and step away from the lady," Frost said, sensing the man was foolish enough to strike a woman in front of witnesses.

Without warning, he found himself the focus of the lady's ire. Her eyes were indeed a fascinating hazel color, an olive green trimmed with rings of gold. There was an inner fire in those clear, intelligent depths that, at the moment, conveyed her fury at his interference.

"Are you a constable?" she asked, her eyes narrowing with disdain.

The absurd question rendered him speechless. How had he become the villain? Finding his tongue, he replied with a question of his own. "Am I dressed like one? No. I am—"

"I do not care who you are, sir," she said, dismissing his attempt at an introduction with a wave of her hand. "What I care about is to remove this child from that blackguard."

Satisfied that she had put Frost in his place, she turned to address the man who had truly earned her wrath. "Release her, and allow us to leave unmolested, and I shall not report you to the proper authorities."

"Katie is my daughter," he shouted at her. "She

stays with me. Leave now, or I'll report you for kidnapping."

"Kidnapping?" The redhead glanced at the girl. "Does he speak the truth? Is he your father?"

The girl quivered like a frightened rabbit. She cast a wary glance at the lady and then at the man who gripped her arm. "He is—was married to my mum."

"I raised the girl as if she were my own," the man said.

The woman ignored him. "And your mum?"

"Dead. Almost a fortnight," the girl said, her eyes filling with tears. "We couldn't afford the medicine she needed."

The redhead shook her head. "Say no more. You have my sympathies." She inhaled deeply as if to fortify her courage. "Do you want to stay with this man?"

"And what choice does she have, I ask you?" he asked, tugging on the girl's arm. "I'm her da, and the only family she has left."

Frost silently concurred. Whatever circumstances transpired before his arrival, the girl belonged with the man who raised her. It was not his concern. Nor the well-meaning lady's.

His fingers lightly grazed the redhead's arm, and she stiffened at his touch. "It is best to stay out of family squabbles."

She glared at him from over her shoulder. "Is that what you think this is? A family squabble? That man has been selling his daughter's . . . er, favors to every gentleman within earshot."

He was not surprised by the lady's outrage. Her sheltered upbringing had not prepared her for the harsh realities poverty had to offer. "May I speak to you privately?"

Her eyes narrowed with suspicion at his request. "Surely, you jest. We are standing in the middle of the street and are surrounded by onlookers."

Frost unceremoniously seized the redhead by the arm and dragged her away from the man and his stepdaughter. He scowled at the man, and stabbed his walking stick in the man's direction. "Do not attempt to flee with the girl. You will not enjoy the consequences." He glanced down at the woman, who was trying to shake off his grip. "Come along, my dear. Let's have our private chat."

Emily struggled to free herself, but it was an act of futility. The gentleman held her as effectively as an iron manacle. If she could have moved her arm, she would have brought the top of her parasol down on his boot. "You have no right to touch me!" she said through clenched teeth as she seethed.

They had only stepped a few yards away from the girl and her beastly stepfather. She glared impotently at him. He was whispering something to poor Katie; most likely, he was threatening her with a beating if she did not stand with him.

"Are you listening to me?"

Emily reluctantly glanced up at her captor. It was the first time she had bothered to truly look at him. He was a gentleman. She had deduced as much with just a passing glance. His manner of speech, clothing, and arrogance marked him as part of the aristocracy.

What stunned her into silence was the beauty of him. If angels walked the earth, they would possess such compelling perfection. His face looked like the work of a sculptor. Unblemished skin, a strong jaw, full lips and brow that age had improved upon. He looked about thirty years old. Despite the hint of tan darkening his skin, his face was unlined. Oh, and his eyes—an intense turquoise-blue that seemed to peer into her very soul. She felt the impact of his stare and wondered if she would see those eyes in her dreams this evening.

"He is going to run off with her," she fretted.

The man gave her an exasperated look. "For all practical purposes, the man is her father. He has every right to run off with her."

"You don't understand," she began, sensing she had been pulled aside for a lecture.

"No, my lovely lady, you do not seem to comprehend the situation," he said sternly, his fingers biting into her arm. He kept his voice low for her ears alone. "If a constable wandered by, he is likely to haul you off to the magistrate for trying to kidnap the girl from the only family she has left. What are you hoping to accomplish? That she is abandoned and placed in a workhouse?"

"A workhouse is better than living with that filthy beast," she whispered back. "Are you aware what he was doing before you came along? Do you even care?"

"I wager more than you do, little innocent," he shot back, frustration and impatience threading his voice. "Hungry bellies need to be filled, and there are unpalatable ways to fill them. Just because you do not like how these people go about—"

Had she mentally described him as an angel? Mayhap a fallen one. "I am not blind to the harshness of the world, sir! I understand that some people are willing to sell their bodies to survive."

"Not willing," he countered. "Willingness has nothing to do with it, when one's choices are made out of desperation. And you have no right to condemn them."

Aghast, she would have staggered backward if she could have stepped away from him. "Is that what you think I am doing? Judging them?" A wave of heat suffused her face. "That girl is not a whore. Her stepfather was selling her virginity to anyone who would meet his price."

The gentleman hesitated. "And you know this for a fact?"

"The man approached my brother. When I saw the girl's face—" She swallowed, and shook her head. Why was she trying to justify her actions? He had no right to judge *her.*

The fear and desperation she had glimpsed in young Katie's eyes had been Emily's undoing. It would have been simpler if she had looked away and continued up the street with her brother. At least she would not be arguing with *him.*

Something akin to pity softened his harsh expression. "You can't save everyone," he said quietly.

"I wasn't trying to save everyone," she said, her eyes stinging with the threat of tears as her sister's face flashed in her mind. "I was trying to save her. What was I supposed to do? Pretend that I didn't see her?"

"Most people would have," he replied, his gaze never leaving her face. "It would have been the simple thing to do."

"Perhaps for you," she said, feeling her temper rise at the thought that her companion would have walked away from the girl or, worse, might have purchased her for an amusement. "I could not turn away when she asked for my help."

"Christ!" he muttered irreverently. "You are one of those kinds of ladies."

"I beg your pardon?"

He waved a dismissive hand in the air. "You're one of those drawing room reformers who dream of ridding the world of its social ills. Allow me to spare you years of lost time and grief. You will not succeed. Evil thrives alongside good. It has from the beginning."

His words cut her to the quick. "You know nothing about me or my intentions." Emily glanced up to check on the man and his stepdaughter, only to note with dismay that they were no longer standing across from them. "Good grief! Release me, he is getting away!"

She kicked him in the shin and gained her freedom. Cursing, the gentleman was at her heels when she spotted the man and girl at the edge of the crowd—but he reached them before her, since her pace was hindered by her skirt and petticoat. The gentleman seized the other man by the coat, leaving Emily to appreciate his agility and strength as she attempted to catch her breath.

While the man blustered on about his innocence, she walked over to the cowering girl and put her arm around her waist. "He will not cause you any more trouble. Are you ready to leave?"

"He will kill me if I defy him," the girl whispered, not taking her eyes off her stepfather.

"You already have," Emily said, silently applauding as the gentleman lifted the man off his feet. An impressive feat of strength, indeed, since the man was clearly heavier. The gentleman allowed his opponent to dangle helplessly for a minute before he released him. The girl's stepfather landed on his backside on the street.

Furious that the nobleman had gotten the better of him, he lashed out with his foot. The stranger nimbly avoided the clumsy attack. Espying the girl standing beside Emily, he pointed his finger at them.

"You there, all of this is your fault, you haughty bitch," he raged at Emily as he climbed to his feet. "If you had kept your nose out of my business, me and my girl would have made a tidy profit by now. I should—"

The gentleman slapped the side of his walking stick against the man's chest, preventing him from taking another step toward her. "Are you threatening the lady? Quite unwise with all of these witnesses about."

His eyes mere slits, he gave the nobleman a dismissive glance. "And what is it to you, or anyone here? Are you planning to take on the responsibility of my Katie? Feed her? Put clothes on her back?" When the gentleman remained silent, the man snorted. "Or maybe you hope the little wench will be so grateful, she will let you plow her for free."

"You are a horrid man!" Emily shouted, earning an angry glance from both men.

Bursting from the crowd, her brother rushed forward. "Emily!"

She was enveloped in her younger brother's arms, and quickly released. "Did you find a constable?"

"One is coming, Em, I swear," he said, sounding breathless and excited. "He told me to run ahead and look after you." He cast a nervous glance at the girl. "And her."

A woman shrieked in fright as the man tried to punch the gentleman. Emily turned in time to see the gentleman avoid the other man's fist while driving his own into his opponent's soft belly.

"Bastard," the injured man wheezed, before he lunged at his attacker and a full brawl broke out that included some of the spectators.

"Come on," Emily said sharply. She grabbed her brother and the girl. "It is time to leave."

Katie followed them willingly, but concern clouded her countenance. "Where will I go? What shall become of me?"

Emily's pace slowed as she considered her choices. When she had stepped in to assist the girl, she had not thought beyond separating her from her abuser. Even the arrogant gentleman had warned her that there were few options for the girl if she left her stepfather. She could not bring her home. Or could she? While her father might understand, she doubted her mother would be pleased by her initiative.

"Do not worry," she said, bestowing a reassuring smile on the young woman. "We will figure something out."

Emily gasped as a firm hand clasped her on the shoulder. She whirled about to confront the person who had the audacity to put his hands on her, and was dismayed to see the dark-haired gentleman again.

"You again?"

The roguish grin he gave her was unsettling. "Aye, me again. Running off? You disappoint me, Emily. I thought you were raised properly."

"You have no right to speak to my sister with such familiarity." Her brother stepped protectively in front of her. "You may address her as Miss Cavell or not at all."

The gentleman brought his hand to his chest. "You wound me. And here I thought we were becoming good friends," he lightly mocked. "Nor have you inquired after my injuries, which I earned on your behalf."

Guilt nibbled at her indignation. "Are you hurt?"

"Preparing to rescue me as well, sweet?" he queried, sounding amused. "Well, don't fret. A few bruises will not force me into bed. Unless you are willing to play nursemaid."

"I certainly will not!" she huffed. No one had ever dared to speak to her in such a manner.

"Stop speaking to my sister," her brother ordered harshly, even though he was aware that he could not best the man in a fight.

"Or you will do what?" the gentleman replied with silky menace. Her brother held his ground, but everyone heard the audible click in his throat as he nervously swallowed. "I thought as much. Nothing but an adorable puppy. Knock on my door when you have grown some teeth."

"Did the constable arrest my stepfather?" the girl asked, drawing the gentleman's attention away from Emily's brother.

The man sighed. "Yes. And he will have a few companions, so you don't have to worry about him getting lonely."

Emily belatedly realized that she owed this gentleman a small measure of gratitude for interfering when he had. The man would have slipped away with this stepdaughter if the stranger had not caught him. "I have been remiss in thanking you, sir. You are a hero."

The compliment did not please him. "Not in the slightest, dear lady. And the name is Chillingsworth. Lord Chillingsworth."

Emily smiled weakly at him. Not only a gentleman, but a titled one as well. He was exactly the type of man her mother would warmly welcome into her drawing room, which was precisely why she hoped the two would never meet. "Well, you have our gratitude regardless, Lord Chillingsworth." She nodded to Katie. "Shall we go? The carriage isn't far."

"No," Lord Chillingsworth said, halting their attempts to depart.

She raised her brows in silent query.

"Forgive my bluntness, Miss Cavell. What are your plans for this girl?" he asked. The mocking amusement he had not bothered to disguise had vanished from his voice.

"We are still making plans," she said defensively.

"As I tried to explain earlier, while your intentions are noble, your inexperience with such matters might place this girl in a worse predicament," he said, those intriguing turquoise-blue eyes of his pinning her in place.

"I intend to help her, Lord Chillingsworth," she said coldly.

He nodded at her brother. "The puppy and the lamb," he chuckled humorlessly.

"You insult us, my lord!" she said, knowing the confrontation with the stepfather could have been handled better.

"Just pointing out the obvious, Miss Cavell." He stared at the girl, but what he was thinking was anyone's guess. "I will take her," he said abruptly.

This was an unexpected development. "What? Uh, no, I cannot allow you—"

He brushed her protests aside and spoke directly to Katie. "I am acquainted with people who are familiar with your circumstances. With their assistance, you will have food, a place to sleep, and prospects."

The wary hope in her eyes diminished as she considered his generous offer. "You are taking me to a brothel."

Before Emily could express her indignation over the suggestion, Lord Chillingsworth was shaking his head.

"No. If that was my intention, I would have left you in your father's care. It would have been simpler, do you not agree?" At her nod, he explained. "You are not the first girl my friends have helped. However, I recommend that you make your decision swiftly. We have drawn too much attention and I would prefer not to linger."

"I'm ready," Katie said. With only an ill-fitting dress that likely belonged to her dead mother, she was willing to put her trust in a man she had just met.

Emily glanced at the girl, mentally debating if she should be upset or relieved that Lord Chillingsworth was prepared to take responsibility for Katie. She was also a tad embarrassed that she had been so ill-prepared to help.

Noting her discomfort, he said, "I promise, my friends are respectable people. She will be in good hands, Miss Cavell. More capable ones than you or I are equipped with."

Emily nodded, fighting down her resentment. She embraced the girl. "You recall the address that I told you? Yes? Excellent. I will be residing in London for a few months. Send me a note when you are settled."

The girl pulled away. "I will. Thank you, Miss Cavell."

She nodded and stepped back. It was silly, but she felt like weeping. "My brother and I—we should be going."

"A moment, Miss Cavell," Lord Chillingsworth called out to her. "Is there a reason why your name is familiar to me?"

"Perhaps you have heard of my father?"

"It is possible. Well, no matter. It will come to me eventually," he said, shaking his head. "By the by, you've neglected to give me your address. I will need it if you wish for me to update you on the girl's well-being."

Emily bit her lower lip to hide her smile. "Reveal my residence to a stranger? That would be unwise, do you not agree, Lord Chillingsworth? Beside, Katie already knows how to find me."

Frost's mouth quirked as the redheaded Emily strolled out of his life as quickly as she had entered it. "I don't think Miss Cavell likes me." Granted, she was a sensible young lady. After all, he was not to be trusted.

His companion giggled. "Maybe you should ask your friends for advice on how to court a lady."

He sighed dramatically. "A useless exercise, my dear Katie. I have no intention of courting anyone—especially a difficult lady like Miss Cavell."

Chapter Five

"Rumor has it, you are flirting with ladies who are half your age, Frost," Vane teased as he leaned back in his chair so he could prop up his feet on the table.

Frost grimaced, not particularly amazed that his good deed had reached his friend's ears. "You must have called on the Sainthills recently."

Four days had passed since he'd presented young Katie to Lady Sainthill. Although it was rarely discussed, the beautiful marchioness had lived as notoriously as the Lords of Vice under a different name—Madame Venna. Before her marriage, she had been the proprietress of the Golden Pearl, one of the most extravagant brothels in London. By using a half-mask to conceal her face and altering her voice, she had amassed a small fortune while keeping her identity a secret. The Lords of Vice had often patronized her establishment.

Those days were behind Catherine, and the less said, the happier Saint was: He was very protective of his lady. Nevertheless, she had old friends whom she trusted and influential new ones. Katie was not the first girl Catherine had found a new home for, nor would she be the last.

"So you have no plans to keep her?"

Frost crossed his arms and stared down at Vane. "What sort of miscreant do you take me for? The poor girl was in trouble and I offered my assistance. Nothing more."

Dare and Reign entered the room. Overhearing part of his explanation, Reign clapped a hand on Frost's shoulder as he passed by him.

"You did a good thing, gent. If not for you, that girl would have come to a bad end," Reign said, moving to the other side of the table.

"I beg of you, no more," Frost pleaded, uncomfortable with the praise. "Next you will be claiming that I possess a heart and insist on naming your sons after me."

Dare chuckled and reached over to smack him on the back of the head. "I did name my son after you, you ungrateful arse!" He took the seat next to Frost.

"It only proves that you have good taste," Frost said genially. "Bishop is a strong given name."

"So why did Sin call this meeting?" Vane asked, yawning into his hand.

"Trouble, gents," Hunter announced. He was not alone. Sin and Nox's steward, Berus, followed in his wake.

"What sort of trouble?" Frost asked. "Has something happened here at Nox?"

It was Sin who replied. "Were you not paying attention last week when Berus was telling us about Halward?"

Frost shrugged. "Colin Halward. So what? The man is trying to build a nasty reputation for himself in London. He's not the first."

Nor would he be the last.

"Trying? Succeeding is more like it."

Before Sin could explain why this Halward fellow had him so bothered, Saint dashed into the saloon. "Forgive my tardiness. It couldn't be helped. What have I missed?"

"Not much. Sin was about to tell us why we should care about Colin Halward," drawled Frost.

"Halward is a first-rate bastard. A few years ago, he caused trouble at the Golden Pearl by attacking one of the girls. It was one of the reasons why Catherine decided to close the establishment." At Frost's blank expression, Saint growled in frustration. "Were you even listening when we discussed the man last week?" he asked, sounding breathless as he sat down on the opposite side of the table.

Frost rolled his eyes. "I might have slept during the boring parts of Sin's rambling lecture."

Maybe he had been distracted during their last meeting. He had made plans to spend the evening with a pretty blonde who had caught his eye.

"Then permit me to remind you that Halward poses a problem to Nox. The bastard views the gambling hell as ripe for the picking since we have not been looking after our interests as closely as we have in the past."

Translation: His six very married friends had preferred to spend their evenings entertaining their wives rather than ending the day at Nox. For years, night after night, they had gambled, fought, drunk brandy and wine until they were half blind, and whored until the wee hours of dawn.

Those wonderful days had begun to fade when Sin had encountered Juliana in Lady Lettlecott's garden. Not that he blamed the lady—overly much.

"And why, I ask, have we not been looking after our interests?" Frost couldn't resist asking.

"Here we go again," muttered Vane, rubbing his face with his hands.

"Berus has done an upstanding job looking after Nox, Frost," Hunter said, his brow furrowing in a manner that proved he was serious. "You insult him to imply otherwise."

"My apologies, Berus," Frost said, acknowledging the man who stood quietly at the door. "Your service to the Lords of Vice has been irreproachable. I have no quarrel with you, my good man."

"Thank you, milord," Berus said, his voice slightly gruff with emotion. "It has been a pleasure serving all of you."

Sin leaned forward, his eyes glittering with anger. "Aye, Frost, we all know the direction of your feelings. You have hardly been subtle or clever about it."

"You wound me, old friend." This was not the first time he and Sin had clashed over Juliana or Nox. His folded his hand into a fist and rubbed his knuckles with his other hand. "Next time, I will be more direct."

"Gentlemen, we did not come here to fight," Reign said, his gaze conveying a direct message that Frost should back off. "We are at fault for not addressing some of these problems sooner. Berus has dealt with threats from Halward, and there has been damage to the property. We have nothing to take to the police, but I concur with Sin and Hunter. The man bears watching."

"And then there is the woman," Hunter added.

"What woman?"

Dare asked before Frost could speak. He settled back into his chair. As much as he would have enjoyed punching Sin, he would have regretted it later.

"Were you not introduced to her at Lady Sellar's ball?"

Dare sent him a puzzled glance. "No. Who is she?"

"A barrister's daughter, I hear," Sin replied. "She has connections to Lord and Lady Tobin. A distant cousin, perhaps."

"I believe her older sister was betrothed to Leventhorpe," Saint said.

The Lords of Vice had turned into a bunch of gossips. "And you know this, how?" Frost asked, not caring one way or the other about the unknown chit.

"Balls. A wealth of information can be gleaned if one has the patience," Sin admitted.

Frost smiled. "I don't."

Raising his hands in surrender, Sin shook his head. "The increased crime around King Street has not gone unnoticed by the *ton*. There has been growing concern about the violence, and many blame the local taverns, brothels, and gambling hells."

"This Cavell woman has been suggesting to all who will listen to her rants that certain establishments are encouraging the criminals. Nox has been mentioned several times." Saint paused, allowing the news to sink in. "Unfortunately, people are beginning to listen to her."

"Cavell." Frost tasted the word on his tongue. Where had he heard that name—wait—no, it could not be! "You do not mean Miss Emily Cavell?"

"Do you know that sharp-tongued redhead?" Sin asked in disbelief.

Frost clapped his hands together and laughed until his ribs ached. His friends looked on, their expressions revealing that they collectively thought he had lost his mind. Miss Emily Cavell. So the lady had picked up her sword and was seeking another battle. How splendid! The Fates certainly had a sense of humor to bring that particular female back into his life. Now that a child's life was not at risk, he intended to enjoy himself.

"Leave Miss Cavell to me, gents," Frost said, ignoring several snorts of disbelief. "As you all know, I have a weakness for redheads."

Emily held her breath as she climbed the staircase of the family's town house. So far, she had managed to enter the house unnoticed, and if her luck held she would have time to change her dress before her mother sent someone to her bedchamber.

She was halfway down the passageway before she was stopped by her mother's voice drifting from the drawing room.

"Emily? Is that you, dear?"

Emily froze, silently debating whether she should

answer. Her mother might dismiss her as one of the servants if she remained quiet. She stared at the green oilcloth beneath her feet, the distinct scent of varnish overpowering the large bouquet of flowers that had been placed on the table at the top of the stairs.

"If this is a game, Emily, I have no time for such nonsense," her mother said, sounding mildly annoyed. "Come join us in the drawing room."

On a wordless sigh, Emily reversed her steps and crossed the threshold into the drawing room.

"Good afternoon, Mother," Emily said cheerfully, bestowing a kiss on the cheek her mother offered. "I was not aware we had a visitor."

"I do not consider Leventhorpe a visitor. As far as I am concerned, he is family and will always be treated as such."

"Madam, you honor me," he said warmly. His gaze shifted to Emily. "Miss Cavell. How is it that you grow even lovelier with each passing year?"

Emily acknowledged his flattery with a smile, and instantly forgave him for his tiny falsehood. As her mother had often told her, she was not the great beauty her sister had been. She had passable looks, though she doubted the earl would have noticed her if not for her connection to his beloved Lucy. She curtsied. "Lord Leventhorpe, it is good to see you again. It is a pity you have been unable to visit Riddlesden."

Riddlesden was the small country house her father had purchased from a desperate marquess the year before he had proposed to her mother. It was the only home she had known. She had spent her tender years there, chasing after her older sister, Lucy, and looking after her younger siblings.

The earl bowed. "I was just offering my apologies to your mother," he said, looking properly contrite. "I confess duty has kept me from visiting your family."

"It is difficult to remain vexed when you are standing before us hearty and hale." She gestured for the gentleman to sit. "Dare I hope you will be remaining in London for a few months?" her mother asked, while beckoning with her hand for Emily to sit beside her.

It was useless to argue, so she sat down on the sofa. Lord Leventhorpe chose one of the chairs. Emily could almost hear the wheels and cogs turning in her mother's head. One thing was certain: The woman was up to something. After Lucy's death, her mother had avoided everything and everyone who had reminded her of her eldest daughter—including the earl. He was living proof of all her mother had lost.

Emily had assumed Lord Leventhorpe had similar feelings about her family. His infrequent visits had waned with the passing years. No one blamed him. The poor man had been devoted to Lucy. He had been inconsolable when news of her death had reached him.

Grief no longer darkened his spirits. With a critical eye, Emily could see why her sister was so taken with him. The forty-year-old looked as fit as any gentleman in his twenties. The ladies of the *ton* were probably quite taken with his quiet demeanor, the distinguishing touch of silver at his temples, and his good looks.

Their gazes met, and he grinned at her affectionately. He would have been her brother-in-law, and she supposed he still viewed her with a brotherly fondness.

"Yes," he replied, straightening his posture as if his physique truly shouldered the weight of his news. "As a matter of fact, I will be established in town for several months. And you?"

Her mother fluttered and preened when his gaze returned to her. "How fortuitous! We have decided to extend our stay as well. Mr. Cavell and I have high hopes for our Emily."

"Me?" she squeaked, flustered to be the center of attention. This was her sister's realm, not hers.

Understanding lit the earl's gaze. "Ah, you hope to introduce our Emily to polite society." He gave Emily a sympathetic glance. "It is expected. How old are you? Nineteen?"

"Twenty, my lord," Emily replied, feeling the heat of a blush on her cheeks. She was not quite a spinster, but most ladies her age had already enjoyed several jaunts to London. If a lady possessed beauty and wealth, her future was often secured during her first season.

Emily was too sensible to believe that she would be as fortunate as her sister had been during her first stay in London when she fell in love with Lord Leventhorpe. Lucy had a romantic, enthusiastic spirit that engaged everyone around her. Emily was a pale shadow in comparison, but she accepted these differences without acrimony.

However, it served her purposes to allow her mother and the earl to believe she was willing to put herself up on the auction block like a horse at Tattersall's. Neither one would approve if they learned the truth.

Lord Leventhorpe opened his arms, the gesture encompassing both women. "Our little Emily is hunting for a husband. Consider me a willing participant. While I have no doubt you have respectable contacts in town, permit me the courtesy of opening a few doors. Never fear, we will secure a respectable husband for her."

Her mother's gaze glistened with joyous tears. "Leventhorpe, your generosity overwhelms me."

Emily was feeling overwhelmed, too.

"If Lucy and I had married, she would have insisted that we look after our Emily" was his quiet admission. "This is the least I can do to honor her memory."

Emily blinked rapidly, her throat tightening as she swallowed. How had she not noticed? Even though five years had passed since her Lucy's death, the earl was still in love with her sister. She could not fathom a man loving her with that kind of devotion.

"Do you think it would be rude of me to compile a list of prospective suitors?" her mother asked, rising from the sofa to ring for the butler.

The question ripped Emily away from her melancholy thoughts. "Uh, Mother . . ." She tried to gain the older woman's attention. "I do not believe a list of suitors is necessary."

"I disagree," Lord Leventhorpe replied. "There are certain gentlemen who are able to claim good breeding, title, and wealth, but they are absolute bounders. Such men are entirely inappropriate for you, my dear."

Accepting that it was an argument that she could not win, Emily nodded and tried not to sulk as the earl and her mother debated about the names that should be added to her mother's list.

Chapter Six

Frost rarely pursued a lady.

First, it took too much effort; more to the point, most were not worthy of the chase. Second, most ladies were willing quarry. His handsome face and title had opened the doors of countless bedchambers—something he had often had taken for granted. However, he had been willing to make an exception for Miss Cavell. Although it galled him to admit it, the lady mildly intrigued him. Her acrimony toward Nox gave him the excuse he needed to seek her out.

In the end, she came to him.

Well, not precisely to him. He and the lady just happened to be attending the same ball this evening. Fate had placed them on the same course, and he was willing to see for himself if the daring Emily was worth all the fuss.

As he watched her from the upper landing, she was blithely unaware of his presence. She was speaking cordially with their hostess, Lady Fiddick, and her niece. Miss Cavell stood out from the trio, looking quite fetching this evening. The fashions this spring tended to favor brighter colors, most of which would have been disastrous for a redhead. Of course, this would not have prevented an ambitious miss who insisted on wearing the latest styles and colors. Unlike her two companions who were draped in scarlet and geranium, Miss Cavell seemed almost subdued in her periwinkle dress. Instead, the observer's eye was drawn to her dark red hair. Her maid had curled the lady's long locks into curls of medium thickness and pinned them into an artful arrangement. Several white roses had been added, and the overall effect made his fingers itch to discover all the hairpins concealed in her thick tresses.

"I recognize that look," a familiar masculine voice drawled behind him. "Only a woman can generate such predatory hunger in a man's gaze."

Frost did not glance at his uninvited companion. "Lord Ravens. I did not realize you strayed from your personal house of iniquity to dally with the civilized."

The earl's amusement covered him like the comforting warmth of a blanket. He had known the man for years. Before Saint's marriage, he and Frost had been frequent guests at Lord Ravens's intimate gatherings of debauchery. Once, the Lords of Vice had even considered inviting the earl to join them. However, not all of his friends appreciated Ravens's unusual appetites, and the subject had been dropped.

Even so, Frost doubted the gentleman would have joined them. He enjoyed being lord and master of his world.

Frost shifted his gaze to Lord Ravens. His mild annoyance faded at the sight of his friend. With hair as dark as his own, the gray-eyed earl looked the same. The twenty-seven-year-old was unmarried and most likely would remain in that state unless he discovered a very understanding wife.

"What brings you here?"

"I could ask the same of you, my friend. After all, you are one of my favorite guests, and yet you have deprived me and my friends of your company."

"My apologies," Frost said sincerely. "My appetites led me elsewhere, and I was content. No offense was intended."

"I am relieved. I value your friendship, and thought Sinclair and your other friends might have persuaded you to abandon our friendship since my gatherings are not for the unenlightened."

Frost heartily agreed. "Then you do not know me as well as you believed. No one, not even my good friends, tells me whom I may spend my evenings with, or where."

Lord Ravens smiled. "Excellent. Then I pray you will return to us soon?"

"How can I refuse such a warm invitation? Especially since I envy the contents of your wine cellar."

The earl coughed into his hand. "And nothing else tempts you?"

Frost laughed. "Oh, there is no doubt that you provide many temptations, gent. It is one of the reasons why some people dislike you."

"Dislike?" He raised his brows as he considered the word. "Several of your friends despise me. Vanewright, in particular, always looks as if he'd like to plant his fist in my jaw."

Vane had not been in the best of moods the last time Saint had dragged their friend to Ravens's town house. It had happened so long ago, it was not worth explaining. Instead, he teased, "You sound surprised. I thought most gents wish to murder you."

Ravens chuckled. "True. Many secretly fear I will steal their wives away from them."

"And would you?"

The earl shrugged. "Is it my fault that I am irresistible to most females?"

Frost clapped a companionable hand on Lord Ravens's shoulder. "And that is why you and I get along so well. We are afflicted with the same problem when it comes to women."

"It is only a problem if you are the man with the unfaithful wife." Ravens casually nodded toward the chattering females below. "And which lady has caught your eye this evening? Or is it all three?"

The question was not meant to unsettle Frost. Lord Ravens was wholly indiscriminate when it came to women or men. Married, virgins, old, and young, he welcomed them all into his bed.

"Why? Do you wish to join me?"

Over the years, there had been evenings when drink, boredom, and lust had turned into a potent combination, and he had indulged in the mindless orgies Ravens had hosted. Frost had rejoiced in the abandonment, but it did not take long for it to pall as well. It was one of the reasons why he had not visited the gentleman's residence in two months.

"Are you willing to share?"

Frost glanced at Emily Cavell. Share her? He did

not like that idea at all. Once he was finished with her, perhaps. For now, he was feeling a little selfish. He wanted to take his time in discovering the lady's secrets, and he was in no mood to turn this into a competition with Ravens. "The decision isn't mine to make. Besides, I've promised Lady Fiddick that I would behave myself. Club business has brought me here."

"Ah, I see. A shame, really," Ravens said, clearly disappointed. "The redhead might prove challenging. Can't see much from our perch, but I'm more interested in what she has hidden underneath her skirt. What do you think? Should I join her downstairs and introduce myself?"

"Why bother?" Frost said, feigning disinterest. "All that pale ivory flesh will bruise too easily, and she likely comes with a disgruntled mother who will sever your cock from your balls if you manage to get it out of your trousers."

Ravens gave him a sharp assessing look, but Frost kept his face carefully blank. His companion must have been satisfied with what he saw, because he slowly nodded in agreement. "Too right. Delicate playthings hold little amusement for me. My preferences lean toward the exotic."

"Naturally," Frost said drily.

"Then I will leave you to your business," Lord Ravens said, bowing formally. "If I encounter some agreeable companions in the ballroom, should I seek you out before I take my leave? We could take them home and fuck them until they no longer can tell which one of us is pounding into them."

Frost shook his head with regret. "Why share the spoils when you can keep them all for yourself?"

"You're a selfish bastard, Frost. It's one of the reasons why I like you." Ravens cast a parting glance at Miss Cavell. "Good hunting."

Am I so obvious?

He was *not* hunting the lady. Not in the manner the earl was implying anyway. Aye, he had every intention of introducing himself to her. He would charm and tease the lady until she lowered her defenses, and then he would find out why she had focused her ire on Nox. The club had nothing to do with young Katie's plight, so she should have no quarrel with the gambling hell. And if he could not soften her opinion on Nox, then he would think of something else. He could offer her a friendly warning that his club was off limits to her crusade.

Or he could seduce her.

Kissing Miss Emily Cavell would be more entertaining than issuing threats. More satisfying, too. He was confident in his skills as a lover. Even an innocent like her would find pleasure in his arms.

Frost grinned at the notion of bedding the lady. He had already made the decision to end his affair with Maryann, and there was no reason why Emily could not take her place in his bed. He could spend the next few months teaching her how to please—

"Fresh hell," he muttered as his gaze narrowed on the four young gentlemen who had surrounded Miss Cavell. There was no doubt in his mind, the seventeen-year-olds were up to mischief and had handpicked their next quarry. Where was Lady Fiddick? She was supposed to be looking after her guest.

I saw her first, gents. She's mine!

The sound of tinkling glass momentarily distracted him, as he noted that a footman carrying a tray of sparkling wine had stepped onto the landing and was heading in his direction.

"May I offer you a glass of wine, milord?" the servant politely inquired.

Frost pressed his lips together as he considered his next move. "I'll take two."

Downstairs, Emily had gained the sudden attentions of four young gentlemen: Lord Macestone, Lord Wilderspin, Lord Ashenhurst, and his twin brother, Lord Boone. They had rattled off their names so quickly, she was not positive if the cheerful blond gentleman standing in front of her was Ashenhurst or Macestone, but at the very least she knew he was the one with a brother.

Emily was usually not so scatterbrained. She had been distracted when they had approached her. Lady Fiddick was expecting her to join her in the ballroom for another round of introductions, but she had begged a moment of privacy. Her plan had been to find refuge in one of the smaller parlors upstairs, but her admirers had cut off her escape.

"How long will you be in London?" one of the brothers asked. She could not tell them apart. They were identical in every aspect, even their waistcoats. Perhaps it was a private game between them to keep everyone guessing which one was which.

"At least a month," she replied, unwilling to give them too many details about herself or her family. These gentlemen were dreadfully sweet, but she deduced that she was older by two or three years.

"What parks have you visited?" the dark-haired one who looked like the youngest of the four queried.

To her left, the one with light brown hair said, "You must take a carriage in Hyde Park."

"You should let us take you," said the blond twin she was beginning to perceive was the leader of their merry band.

Emily glanced at him sharply. "I beg your pardon?"

"Provide escort, he means, Miss Cavell," the gentleman with the brown hair and blue eyes said, this time to the right of her.

When had he switched positions with the other one?

She glanced over her right shoulder. Which one was he? Macestone, Wilderspin, or Ashenhurst? Just keeping an eye on all four of them was making her dizzy.

"It is very generous, but I have family in town," she replied.

Lord Boone looked at her with a guileless expression on his face. "Wouldn't your family be pleased that you are making new friends?"

"Of course they would. That isn't the point," she protested. "Now if you will excuse me, gentlemen, I must return to my friends."

"Tarry with us awhile longer," the blond she decided was Lord Ashenhurst entreated. "The ballroom is too crowded for a decent conversation. Why don't we adjoin to the gardens?"

"A splendid idea," his brother said, moving to stand beside his twin. "It would give us more time to persuade you that our intentions are honorable."

A sudden hiss and sputtered curse from behind made Emily spin around. The action revealed several unpleasant facts. First, she noted that two of her companions had liquid dripping from their faces and hair, and, second, there was an unexpected tug on her skirt. She glanced down and noticed that someone had used fishing hooks and line to tie several old shoes to the hem of her skirt.

This was nothing more than a prank. She glared at the two who had been standing behind her. "How could you!" she said, trying to decide if one or both deserved her anger.

Neither one of them was paying attention to her. In fact, all four of them were looking at the balcony above them. Puzzled, she lifted her gaze—and her lips parted at the sight of Lord Chillingsworth.

"How careless of me," he said, not sounding very apologetic. "Someone might have gotten hurt if the glasses had slipped from my fingers. It would have been tragic if those handsome visages had been scarred."

Lord Boone elbowed his brother. "Do you know who that is?" he whispered.

"Quiet," his brother ordered, staring boldly at the gentleman who had interrupted their fun.

"It's Chillingsworth," replied the dark-haired Lord

Macestone. "Very few men have the courage to face him in a duel or in the ring."

"Ah, I see my notorious reputation has reached the ears of you reckless puppies," Lord Chillingsworth said silkily. "Then you know I have little patience for fools. Apologize to Miss Cavell, and I expect to hear humility in your voices."

All four gentlemen spoke together.

"We beg your pardon, Miss Cavell."

"No offense, miss. It was just a small prank."

"My apologies."

"Our sincerest regrets, Miss Cavell."

Lord Chillingsworth's smile widened. "There now, that wasn't too difficult to swallow. Less so than a man's fist, hmm?" He disappeared from view, and Emily realized to her dismay that the earl was heading for the stairs.

It must have dawned on her male companions as well. The two behind her brushed by her without saying a polite farewell and ran for the nearest door.

"Come on!"

Lord Boone glanced warily at the stairs. "Another time, Miss Cavell. Are you coming, brother?"

Emily was startled to see his twin was staring at her. "I was sincere about the ride in Hyde Park. Preferably without Chillingsworth." The blond's smile turned into a sneer when he saw the earl. He followed his brother and friends out the door.

Lord Chillingsworth did not quicken his long stride as he descended the stairs. To Emily's consternation, instead of pursuing the young gentlemen, he walked up to her. Without being asked, he crouched down and carefully removed the fishing hooks from her skirt. Good grief, Emily had forgotten all about them.

He cast a wintry glance at the empty doorway. "I hope you are not one of those weak-minded females who faint at the first glimpse of blood," he said, probably regretting that he had let the pranksters off so easily.

"Why do you ask? Are you planning to shed any on my behalf?" Until she had arrived in London, there had never been any need for anyone to come to her defense, and this gentleman had done so twice.

Lord Chillingsworth shoved the shoes, hooks, and line under the nearest chair. He stood. "It's tempting, but the prank was harmless. And at their age, my friends and I were—" He did not finish his confession, but instead he offered her a smile that was meant to charm her. "Never mind. I will not bore you with old tales. Why don't I find you another glass of wine, eh?"

He seemed determined to remain at her side. "Why? You dumped the contents of your glass on Macestone and Wilderspin, not mine."

"Macestone and Wilderspin were their names? Good to know."

While she did not appreciate being the target of their prank, she wished them no ill will. Something inside her warned her that Lord Chillingsworth was not as generous. "You are not intending to do anything to those young gentlemen?"

"Me? Not at all. I am just taking an interest in the season's latest litter of brash puppies. That footman with the tray of wine is wandering about upstairs. Shall we seek him out and find you a glass?"

"Hmm." He was attempting to distract her. However, Emily doubted he would share his intentions about the young lords. "I told our hostess that I would follow her into the ballroom."

"And yet, here you are with me," Lord Chillingsworth said, steering her in the opposite direction. "A more exciting choice, do you not agree?"

Chapter Seven

Ignoring her fainthearted protests, Frost managed to get Emily up the staircase, relieve the footman of two more glasses of wine, and distract her with discourse about the Fiddicks, Katie, and the weather so casually that she seemed bemused to find herself seated next to him on the sofa.

The lady did not stand a chance.

Frost could almost pity her, but why bother when her proximity conjured other stimulating emotions.

"So Katie is happy with her new circumstances?" she asked for a second time.

"My dear Miss Cavell, I have no reason to lie to you," he said smoothly. "However if you do not believe me—"

The lady wrinkled her nose as she took a sip of her sparkling wine. It was quite adorable. "Oh, I believe you. I must admit that I felt a tad guilty for leaving the girl in your care when I was the one who promised to help."

"You did assist her," Frost said bluntly. "You

distracted her stepfather from selling her to a less compassionate soul until my arrival. It was enough."

Miss Cavell laughed as she brought her gloved finger to her lips. She lightly stroked her lower lip. If she had been like the other women he usually spent his evenings with, he might have viewed the gesture as an invitation.

"Then Katie and I were most fortunate that you came along when you did," she mused, her hazel eyes gleaming up at him.

"No, Miss Cavell, I am the fortunate one."

She blushed, not misunderstanding his meaning. Alone in the informal parlor and devoid of distractions, Frost took a moment to study her. Emily Cavell was not a beauty in the classical sense. He had encountered and bedded ladies who were lovelier. Nevertheless, the lady was unique, and an educated eye would have described the combination of her features as striking. Her flawless ivory skin on closer inspection did not possess a single freckle. She looked him directly in the eyes, and the lack of coyness was both annoying and refreshing.

Had no one taught the chit how to flirt?

She was tall for a female, but he was taller than most gentlemen at six feet, two inches; the lady had to tilt her head back to meet his gaze. A long, narrow nose, not-too-full lips, and a stubborn chin gave the impression that this was a woman who relied on her intelligence rather than her looks.

"Are you not enjoying the wine?" he asked when she set her glass aside.

"Yes, but it's early and my encounter with those

young gentlemen proved that I need a clear head if I wish to get through the evening without embarrassing my family."

"Your family is in attendance?"

She nodded. "My mother, my younger brother—you have already met Cedric—and his twin sister, Judith."

"And what of your father?"

"Work has kept him from my mother's side." She hesitated. "He is a barrister, and the case he is working on requires all of his attention."

"How fascinating," he murmured, noting that some of the stiffness in her shoulders eased at his reaction. Had she been worried that he would have thought less of her because of her father's profession? "So you are interested in the law as well?"

"Not particularly," she confessed. "Besides, he has Ashley. My older brother is currently studying law so he can follow in our father's footsteps. What about your family? Did they join you this evening?"

Very few people were courageous enough to mention his family. Her curiosity pleased him, so he decided to indulge her. "I arrived alone. My father passed away a long time ago, and my mother . . . suffice to say, she has not been a part of my and my sister's lives for years."

Her face pinched with sympathy. "Forgive me. It is unlike me to pry. I, too, have lost family. My sister. It has been five years, and I am still mourning the loss."

The death of a beloved sibling might explain why they had never met until now. Had Emily buried herself in the country while she grieved for her dead sister? What she needed was someone to disrupt her comfortable world.

That someone was him.

"Now I must apologize for making you sad." He reached forward, deliberately ensuring that his arm would brush against hers as he picked up her wine-glass. "Here. Let us drink. A toast to family lost."

"Very well." Emily gave him a sweet, endearing smile as she accepted the glass he had handed her. She dutifully raised her glass. "To family lost."

Frost touched his glass to hers. "And newly found friends," he said, before drinking. They would become very good friends if he had his way.

And he could not wait to begin.

Impulsively, he leaned closer to kiss her. Women highly praised his kisses, and they tended to be more reasonable when he was pleasuring them.

At the first tentative touch, Emily whispered, "What are you doing?"

Not withdrawing, he whispered back, "Kissing you. Now cooperate."

"I think not." With no place to retreat, she slumped down to avoid his mouth and then rolled to her side so she could stand.

This was not the first time a lady had rejected his advances. During his thirty years, he had encountered a few reluctant ladies who claimed they had not enjoyed his kisses. Since they had gone on to marry his friends, he assumed that they had feigned their dislike out of respect for their husbands.

Telling the truth would have made their frequent gatherings rather awkward.

However, Emily had dismissed him without giving him a chance to prove himself. He set his wineglass down and staggered to his feet. "Why not? What harm is there in a kiss, Emily?"

She rolled her eyes and laughed. "It is Miss Cavell to you, Lord Chillingsworth. Granting you liberty to use my given name will only encourage you."

"And what is wrong with encouraging me?" he asked in reasonable tones.

"Do you want me to make a list?" she replied, while positioning herself behind one of the chairs. "I appreciate what you have done for Katie, and rescuing me from those young—"

"Damn puppies!" he exclaimed with disgust. "You assume I am no better than those arses who cozied up to you for a prank. Someone told you that I am a Lord of Vice."

Emily clutched the high back of the chair. Her gaze shifted from him to the doorway. "A Lord of—what? Did you say *vice*?"

He bit his tongue off before he apologized for a nickname he was not responsible for creating. "Yes. It is silly name I and my six friends have been stuck with since we were—"

"Uh, damn puppies?" Her lips pursed as she fought back a smile. "It is hardly a comforting recommendation to your good character."

Was she teasing him? The realization gave him hope that he had not frightened her off. He slowly approached the chair she was using as a shield until they were face-to-face.

"What if I told you that we deserved it?"

"Then I would assume you and your rebellious cohorts were very bad boys," she said breathlessly.

"Men," he corrected. He pressed his right knee into the thick cushion of the chair so he could close the distance between them. "And yes, we have garnered a certain reputation with the *ton*. However, a few of us have become respectable. They have married and sired heirs."

Emily had courage. Nor did she back away when his mouth was mere inches from hers. "But not you," she said.

Frost shrugged. "Not much point. Someone has to maintain our notoriety. It might as well be me."

His lips twitched in anticipation. He longed to pull her closer and silence her with a thorough, satisfying kiss. When he was finished, everyone would know what mischief the naughty wench had been up to.

"So this business about kissing me. Is this about securing your reputation?"

"Not precisely."

"So how does this work? Do you spend your evening chasing after ladies? Is there a particular number? How many allow you to catch them?"

"No one is letting me *do* anything," he muttered, unhappy with the direction of her questions.

Emily gasped. "Then you force yourself upon them." She leaned closer. "There is a dreadful name for that sort of gentleman, you know. I am amazed

Lord and Lady Fiddick granted you entry into their respectable town house."

"You are cleverly twisting my words, Emily. No one is being forced, damn you!" he snapped, his desire waning into an urge to throttle her. "This is not about the *ton* or the nickname they gave us. Here and now, this is about me and you. Is it wrong of me to want to kiss you?"

Her cheeks warmed to a rosy pink at his declaration. "Yes," she said, drawing away from him. "Because I am not my sister."

Frost did not know how to respond to the nonsensical comment. He had never met her younger sister. "What the devil are you prattling on about?"

"Gentlemen filled the drawing room with flowers, wrote her poetry, and fought duels over her. She was a raving beauty every man longed to kiss. Not I."

"I disagree. If you would stand still, I'll prove it."

"Ah, I see," she said, nodding. "I am the first lady to spurn you."

"No," he said gruffly. "There have been others."

"Hmm . . . too few, in my opinion. You have my sympathies, Lord Chillingsworth." Emily patted him on the cheek and walked away.

The chit was leaving. Frost scrubbed his face. How had she turned the tables on him? Any other woman would have melted in his embrace and begged for him to kiss her again.

She set her empty wineglass down on one of the tables and headed toward the door.

"Wait. A moment, Miss Cavell," he said through clenched teeth since it came close to begging.

Frost charged after her when she refused to halt. He caught up to her just as she stepped out of the parlor. He spun her about; she had to grasp his shoulders to keep her balance.

"We are not finished with our discussion."

Emily glared at him. "Do you know the difference between you and the young lords that you threatened earlier?"

"No. Nor do I care." Snarling at her would not soften her disposition toward him. Where was the charm he was known for? He had yet to ask a single question about her hatred for Nox. Frost took a deep breath. "What is the difference?"

"Only a small one," she said too sweetly. "Your pranks require more sophistication than theirs. Although I believe—mm—ph—"

He used his mouth to silence her. It was the smartest course, since the woman had the ability to castrate a man with her tongue. There were other, more tantalizing and pleasurable uses for the organ.

At first, Emily held her ground. She was as rigid as a board in his arms, and her mouth was as yielding as a threatened clam. Frost had stolen his first taste of her, and he regretted his rough handling. Almost. Her rambling explanation about her sister had revealed that the lady had not been kissed.

He was the first man to experience the passion she kept hidden.

His lips softened against hers and she drew in a ragged breath. Closing his eyes, he breathed in her scent. She smelled faintly of orange blossoms. He kissed her lightly, an unspoken apology for his anger. Emily's response was as generous as her heart. Her lips, unschooled in the art of kissing, parted and beckoned for him to take more.

It was an invitation he could not refuse.

Slowly, he worshiped her mouth. He caressed the plump padding of her lower lip with his lips, using the tip of his tongue as a teasing whip to moisten his path.

When he lifted his head, he stared down into the fathomless depths of her hazel eyes. The green and gold rings glowed with the rising passion she likely did not recognize within her. Unfortunately, Frost was very aware of his body. He was aroused and feeling reckless. A part of him longed to drag her back into the small parlor and lock the door. The Fiddicks' sofa would suffice as he kissed Emily in other delectable areas of her body.

It was the most difficult thing he had ever done, but he released her and stepped back.

"Lord Chillingsworth." Emily stared at him with bemused wonder in her gaze as if she had never truly seen him.

"We have moved beyond formality," he said, pleased that he had figured out a way to sweeten her disposition. "My friends call me—"

"Frost!"

Emily stared at him, her distress apparent. Almost being caught in a torrid embrace with a Lord of Vice had turned her ardor to ash, and she was probably vexed with him again. Annoyance flashed across his expression as he noticed his sister and Dare were to blame for this intrusion. How the devil had they found him? He had not told Regan that he would be attending the ball this evening.

"Regan and Dare, this is unexpected," he said, genially, while his gaze silently ordered them to *go away.*

"Lady Fiddick told us you were here," his sister said, stepping away from her husband to kiss Frost on the cheek. "I told Dare that I would not believe it until I saw you myself."

Dare stood behind his wife with his arms crossed. His attention shifted from Frost to Emily, and there was a question in his gaze. How much had the couple seen? Enough, he assumed.

The bravado Emily had displayed during their argument had left her. She stood quietly beside him, most likely wishing she had escaped before they had drawn spectators.

There was nothing he could do to ease her embarrassment. It was best to get through the introductions. Maybe she wouldn't look so miserable once she learned that they had been interrupted by several members of his family.

"Regan and Dare, I would like to introduce you to—"

His sister brought her hands to her lips. "Emily . . . Emily Cavell. My goodness, is that truly you?"

Frost's eyebrows rose. "You are acquainted with Emily?"

The lady in question frowned at him for using her given name, but she was smiling when she walked toward his sister. "Lady Regan." She curtsied.

"Oh, I will have none of that from you," Regan said, embracing the startled woman.

Puzzled, Emily glanced at him and then his sister. Why was she so surprised that he had a sister? Granted, the resemblance was subtle, but she was looking at him as if he had been hatched by chickens.

"Oh, how are you? I love your dress. Which shop did you use? Will you be staying in London for a few months? Oh, goodness, I cannot believe it is you!" Regan babbled on.

"Nor I." Emily nodded and smiled as she decided which question to address first. She noticed Dare standing behind Regan and must have thought it was too rude to ignore him. "Is this your husband?"

"Yes." His sister extended her hand to Dare, and he joined his marchioness. "Emily, may I present my husband, Lord Pashley."

His friend took Emily's hand and bowed. "A pleasure, Miss Cavell. Our friends call me Dare," he said, clearly amused by his wife's joy over discovering an old friend.

"Emily," she said easily, and Frost was tempted to kick his friend for his gallantry.

"How did you meet my sister?" Frost inquired, his curiosity getting the better of him. Although the Cavell surname was vaguely familiar to him, he could not recall his sister playing with a girl named Emily.

Regan and Dare's arrival had given her an excuse to ignore him, but she could not avoid replying to his question. "Miss Swann's Academy for Young Ladies.

She was four years older, but Regan's exploits were legendary and an inspiration to the other girls."

His sister grinned cheekily at him. "You are kind to say so, Emily, but I highly doubt the other girls were inspired by my antics. In fact, I was in trouble so often Miss Swann ran out of punishments."

Before Frost could press her about the punishments she had failed to mention, Regan grabbed Emily by the hands and said, "Let's go into the parlor and chat awhile. I have so much to tell. Do you recall Nina and Thea? They are in town. We must plan an outing!"

She and Emily entered the parlor, with Regan capable of holding both sides of the conversation. Neither lady gave any thought to the gentlemen. Frost wondered if they were even allowed to join them.

He started to follow, but Dare caught him by the arm.

"You might want to wait," he said enigmatically.

"Why should I?"

Dare's pointed glance at the front of Frost's trouser had him reaching for—Christ, no! He covered the proof of his waning arousal with his hand. Had Emily noticed?

"Splendid. No wonder Emily was gaping at me as if I possessed two heads!"

Dare burst into a fit of laughter.

Frost groaned and pressed his fingers against his eyelids. He chuckled, still able to appreciate the humor of his predicament. "Do you think Regan noticed?"

"Fear not, old friend. It was barely noticeable, and the ladies were distracted."

"Now you are just being cruel," Frost said, disgruntled.

"Stop whining," his brother-in-law said cheerfully. "It is your fault for kissing Miss Cavell in the corridor. Usually you are discreet."

"I am discreet. My intention was to question her, not kiss her," he said, and then recalled that he had never ruled out kissing. He did not believe in denying himself, and now that he had kissed Emily, he wanted to do it again. "She was taking slices out of me with her sharp tongue. Kissing her was a clever defense."

Dare nodded, understanding lighting his gaze. "You did not anticipate liking it, eh?"

"I *always* like it, Dare. I just didn't think I would like it that much," he confessed grumpily.

"Tread carefully, gent. She's Regan's friend and an innocent." His friend held up his hand to silence Frost from issuing an angry retort. "Ravishing innocents brings a man nothing but trouble. Besides, if you break Emily's heart, you will earn your sister's wrath."

"I can handle my sister," Frost replied with confidence. "And I have no plans to bed Miss Cavell. The kiss was an aberration. I will keep my hands off her."

Dare grunted but did not offer his opinion.

Frost was grateful. He often lied, but never to himself.

There was a first time for everything.

Chapter Eight

Lord Chillingsworth was the man called Frost.

In mind-numbing disbelief, she sat next to the man's sister—an older girl she had liked and secretly admired for her courage to stand up to her tormentors—while she struggled to maintain her composure.

Why does it have to be him?

Shouldn't she have sensed that the charming, beautiful man who had swept into her life was the devil in disguise? And then there was Regan. How could she share blood with such a heartless creature?

"How did you meet my brother?" Regan asked.

Emily's attention switched from the doorway, where she only caught a glimpse of Lord Chillingsworth's elbow, back to his sister.

"Ah, well . . ." She cleared her dry throat. "A man was selling his stepdaughter on the streets after her mother died, and I found myself in a bit of trouble when I interfered. Your brother's timely arrival prevented anyone from getting hurt."

"My brother has always loved a good fight," she

said candidly. The affection for her older sibling was evident. "And he abhors bullies."

Emily absently nodded as she glanced again at the doorway. Lord Pashley laughed, but she was too far away to overhear Lord Chillingsworth's response. "He even took responsibility for Katie. He said that he knew someone who could help her."

Regan's reaction put to rest any lingering concern that she might have held for Katie. "He must have approached Catherine for assistance."

"Your brother did not divulge names."

"Catherine is the Marchioness of Sainthill. The lady has some interesting friends," Regan confided, her emerald-and-diamond earrings glittering as she tucked an errant curl behind her ear. "Her husband is one of Frost's friends."

"Is he one of the Lords of Vice?" she asked bitterly. In hindsight, the nickname suited the man called Frost perfectly.

"Yes, as is my husband," she added, noting her friend's frown. "I am surprised my brother mentioned it. Since Hunter's marriage to Grace, he has been rather cranky about the whole subject."

"Why?"

"All of his friends have married," she simply said. "He is the last remaining bachelor, and I often wonder if he feels obligated to maintain their reputation. Dare and the others have considered shutting down Nox, but Frost won't even consider it."

Emily's eyes widened at the club's name. "Nox?"

"When Frost and his friends were younger, they managed to get blackballed from most of the clubs so they started their own. To fund it, they opened a gambling hell. It's quite successful," she said proudly.

Good heavens! "I am certain it is." Emily did not know if she could endure another surprise this evening.

Lord Chillingsworth and his friends were connected to Nox. Why had no one told her? A few weeks ago, when she had condemned the gambling hell to a small group of ladies, everyone had agreed with her. Some of them had even offered their assistance in helping her find a way to shut down the notorious club.

"I need to leave," Emily said abruptly as she stood.

"What?" Regan looked disappointed as she rose from the sofa as well. "It has been years since we have seen each other. Now that I know you will be remaining in town, I want to introduce you to my friends."

"You are too kind," Emily said, immediately regretting how dismissive she sounded.

"Not really."

Her eyes widened in astonishment at the marchioness's admission.

Noting Emily's expression, Regan elaborated, "When Frost banished me to Miss Swann's, I was angry, hurt, miserable, and defiant. Most of the girls either hated me or feared me." Her friend's blue eyes misted as the memories of that period in her life assailed her. "Nina and Thea eased my loneliness, but then there was you. When we first met, I could tell that you were appalled by my behavior, but you still befriended me. I never told you how much I appreciated your kindheartedness."

Although Emily was touched by the marchioness's words, it just added another layer of doubt and complication to her muddled feelings. "I often worried that you considered me more of a nuisance than a friend."

"Never." Regan cast a discreet glance at the doorway. "I hope your leaving has nothing to do with the fact that my husband and I caught you kissing my brother."

Emily's shy smile faded as shame burned throughout her entire body at the thought that her brazen behavior had been on display for anyone to observe. How could she have been so reckless?

"You saw us?" she asked, wishing the conflagration of her mortification would simply turn her into a pile of ash that could be swept away.

"As we made our way upstairs." Regan moved closer and whispered, "I do not wish to speak unfavorably of my brother. Nevertheless, I feel obligated to warn you that he is quite the scoundrel."

"Compliments, brat?" Frost said mockingly as he followed Lord Pashley into the parlor. "You astound me. It is so good to have the support of my family."

An awkward silence settled in the room.

Without meeting the earl's knowing gaze, Emily hastily uttered her farewells and left the room before anyone thought to stop her.

Regan's shoulders slumped with the burden of her guilt. "Frost—"

"Spare me," he snapped, ruthlessly cutting off her apology. He glanced at Dare. If he had seen pity in the gent's face, he would have punched him. "Well, that was an exceedingly unique experience. Usually, when I kiss a lovely wench, she doesn't flee from the room."

Sighing, his sister sat down on the sofa. "Out of fairness, Emily Cavell deserved to be warned. You *are* a scoundrel. And few ladies can resist you when you decide to be charming."

"Why thank you, brat." He sat down beside her and pressed a kiss to her temple. "However, you should credit your friend with more intelligence. She seems immune to my charm."

It was perverse of him, but it only made him want to kiss her again. Whether she was willing to admit it or not, she had liked kissing him.

"Clever girl," Dare teased.

He grinned at his brother-in-law. "Care to wager on it, gent?"

"No wagers," his sister protested. "I consider the lady a friend."

Frost shrugged, content to let the matter drop. "I wouldn't dream of it. Even so, Miss Cavell has not seen the last of me."

With a polite smile pasted on her face, Emily stood beside her mother for the next two hours in the ballroom while she discussed gardening and the proper sauce for halibut with several ladies. During that time, three gentlemen had approached the group and invited her to dance. Much to her mother's disapproval, she had refused all offers. She explained apologetically that she had sprained her foot, and the lie left the gentlemen's pride intact while it spared her a long lecture from her mother. In truth, she had been worried that if Lord Chillingsworth noticed that she was dancing, he might approach her again. Thankfully, he had kept his distance. She had only caught a glimpse of him once as he and Lord Pashley had made their way to the card room. Instead of relief, dread pooled in her stomach.

I kissed Frost.

Emily shuddered and told herself it was in disgust. Hours later and alone in her bedchamber, she could still feel him. Her lips tingled as if he had branded her. Standing in front of her mirror dressed in her nightgown, she moistened her lower lip and tasted him.

She had barely spoken a word on the drive home. Her mother and younger siblings managed to carry on a conversation without her. They thought she was weary from their evening out, so when her mother told her to go to bed, Emily kissed her on the cheek and dutifully went upstairs. Mercy had been waiting for her when she entered her bedchamber. The maid looked after her and her sister Judith, and when she wasn't needed she was given other chores by their housekeeper. Mercy helped her undress, and when Emily could manage on her own, the maid slipped out of the room to check in on Judith.

Turning away from the mirror, she grabbed her hairbrush from the dressing table and walked over to her bed. She sat down on the edge of the mattress and brushed her hair. Occasionally, she paused to pluck a hairpin that Mercy had missed, but it did not take long before her strokes were unhindered from crown to the ends of her hair.

Emily was too distracted by the events of this evening to find pleasure in the task. When she was a child, Lucy used to brush Emily's hair each night. However, her sister had to catch her first. This often involved Lucy pushing her to the ground and sitting on her back. Emily retaliated by pulling her sister's hair. Once the yelling and name-calling had ceased, the pair had settled down and focused on the task.

They talked about their day. They shared their joys, the real and imaginary slights—usually their brother Ashley was to blame—and their discoveries. In hindsight, Emily had been too young to appreciate those unguarded moments with her sister.

Lucy often complimented Emily's red hair, declaring it her best feature. Naturally, she had envied her sister's golden-blond tresses, similar in hue to their mother's. Her red hair was a legacy from some unknown ancestor, and as a child she considered it too garish to be pretty. She had longed for hair like her sister's.

Lucy.

Not all of her recollections of her sister were happy. She recalled one afternoon when Lucy had been furious at her for eating the last gooseberry tart. She called Emily a red-haired changeling. Six years old at the time, she had thought it an unforgivable insult. She had sobbed in her mother's arms for almost an hour, and her sister had been sent to bed without supper as a punishment.

When her parents had sent her off to Miss Swann's Academy for Young Ladies, Emily had begged them not to. It had seemed frivolous to be acquiring the social polish reserved for noblemen's daughters and heiresses. She blamed her mother for the decision. As Viscount Ketchen's youngest daughter, she expected her daughters to eventually make respectable matches even though they were commoners. Although her mother's life no longer revolved around the *ton,* she had high hopes that one of her girls would marry a nobleman.

By the time Emily had returned home, it was obvious that their mother had placed all her hopes in her eldest daughter. Lucy's first season in London had been a success. Using the family's connections, her sister had been presented to members of some of the most influential families in England. And while the Earl of Leventhorpe was not the only gentleman to fall in love with her sister, he had been one of the richest. His offer had been overly generous, and her parents eagerly accepted.

Emily had assumed that her sister was overjoyed by the prospect of marrying Lord Leventhorpe. Her letters from London implied she was enjoying herself, and she had made dozens of friends. Eventually, Emily had traveled to London for a visit. She had been too young to join her sister as she made the rounds to the countless fetes and balls, but there were other amusements to entertain her.

Lucy had changed.

Even now, she struggled to accept it. Emily did not know if the years they had spent apart had altered their friendship or if London had ruined her. Something had changed her sister.

Or someone.

Emily stopped brushing her hair. If she persisted she would end up bald, and then her mother would make her wear those unattractive headdresses many matrons preferred. She set down the hairbrush and used the bedpost for support as she climbed to her feet.

Pressing her face against the carved wood, she groaned. "He can't be the one. Lucy was confused. She did not know what she was saying at the end."

Emily could not avoid the truth. She had come to London to find a man named Frost, but he had found her first. He had even rescued her and a young girl.

I feel obligated to warn you that my brother is quite the scoundrel.

Regan's words had haunted her all evening. She had erroneously assumed her sister's seducer had been a Lord Frost or a Mr. Frost. She had not considered that the name Lucy had whispered in her ear with her last breath might be an affectionate nickname.

There was no one watching her. She no longer had to hide her feelings. With a muffled sob, Emily did not bother hold back her tears. Her hands slid down the bedpost as she fell to her knees. She cried for her sister, who had loved the wrong man and had taken her life because she could not live with her sins. She also cried for herself. Lucy had asked Emily to keep her secrets, and she had kept her promise.

However, the knowledge that the man who had seduced and abandoned her sister had walked away unscathed had weighed on her heart. Her guilt and frustration had burned like a caustic poison in her throat. It was only when her mother had told her that she would be spending the season in London that a kernel of a plan began to germinate.

What if she could find Frost?

What would it take to destroy him?

It was a fanciful notion. She was a mere woman. If he was a nobleman, what power could she wield against him? Or worse, what if he was a dangerous man?

The Frost she had met on the streets of London fit both descriptions. What troubled her most was that she was attracted to the earl. He was handsome and witty, and he was the first man Emily had kissed.

Sitting on the floor of her bedchamber, Emily sobbed as if her heart were broken. She barely knew the man, but if he was the gentleman who ruined her sister, then he was her enemy.

She did not want to make the same mistake as her sister, and fall in love with Lord Chillingsworth.

Chapter Nine

Frost was in a foul mood when he entered his town house.

Emily Cavell had literally slipped from his fingers before he was finished with her; Dare had teased him mercilessly all evening; the damn puppies he had chased away from Emily had taken turns sneering at him—though they were intelligent enough to keep their distance; he had lost at cards; Lady Netherley tried to corner him because there was a young lady that the elderly marchioness thought he should meet; and an old rival had worked up the courage to confront him about a former lover. Frost assured the gentleman that he was happy to oblige him, but not in the middle of Lord and Lady Fiddick's ballroom. As he had departed to confront the man in a less public setting that they had arranged in advance, his sister told him to stay away from Emily.

"No lady holds your heart for long," she had pointed out as they stood in the Fiddicks' front hall. "And I will not have you breaking my friend's."

"I cannot break something I have never claimed

or desired" had been his reply. "My interests lay farther south."

It had been the wrong thing to say to Regan. With her nose in the air, she had stomped off. Dare would eventually calm her down with assurances that her friend was safe from Frost's machinations.

Some lies benefited everyone.

"Good evening, Lord Chillingsworth," his butler greeted him in the front hall. Several lamps were lit, but his state of undress revealed the servant had been roused from his bed.

"Sparrow, there is no need for you to wait on me at this late hour," Frost chided as he removed his gloves. If his servants kept his unpredictable evening hours, nothing would ever get done during the day.

He walked over to the small mirror on the wall and peered at the small cut at the corner of this mouth. The bleeding had stopped almost immediately, but the wound was tender.

"Milord, you are hurt."

"It is nothing. Lasher has the pugilist skills of an elderly woman. If his fingernail hadn't scratched me, I would have walked away from the fight unscathed."

"I have every faith in your abilities," the butler said soothingly. "But there is no reason to risk it becoming infected. I will heat some water to clean it properly."

"There's no need to trouble yourself, Sparrow. A glass of brandy before I retire should clean it to your satisfaction." He turned his back on his reflection and headed toward the stairs. "Once you've brought the brandy, you may return to your bed."

"One more thing, milord." The butler glanced upstairs. "A lady has come to call on you."

Frost scowled at the news. "And you let her in? What could she have promised to convince you to defy my standing orders?"

He had very few rules when it came to his mistresses. Most of them were negotiable, but one rule he refused to yield on. He conducted his affairs anywhere but his private residence. While it would have been convenient to invite his lovers into his town house, he had Regan to consider. As a girl, she had always been curious, had asked too many questions, and had observed too much in her young life. It had been one of the reasons why he had sent her to Miss Swann's Academy. Even though he had tried to shield her from witnessing the baser needs of the Lords of Vice, she had grown into a cheeky little minx.

"Is it Lady Gittens?" he asked, dreading the confrontation with his former mistress. He supposed it would be rude for him avoid the lady and send Sparrow upstairs to escort her out.

"No, milord." Frost's relief was brief when the servant added, "It's *her.* I tried, but I could not persuade her to call on you at a proper time."

So she had finally sought him out. After meeting Miss Cavell, and then later calling on the Sainthills to assist him with Katie, he had forgotten about the meeting that had brought him to the area that day.

Frost sighed. No, he did not blame Sparrow. The lady upstairs never listened to anyone, and that included him. "You did your best. Now go to bed. I'll deal with her."

As he climbed the stairs he tried to recall the last time he had seen her. Was it two years or three? Not that it mattered. She was a shrewd wench. When she wanted something from him, she always managed to find someone to act as her messenger.

The drawing room door was open. Had she been eavesdropping on his conversation with Sparrow, or was she simply waiting for him to return home?

He crossed the threshold and noted that she had made herself at home. She sat in one of his favorite chairs while she sipped his brandy. The passing years had been kind to her, he thought, as he studied her impassively. Her hair was as dark as his own. If time had added a touch of gray, he could not see it at this distance. She had painted her face to hide her age, but it was subtle and suited her coloring. Once he had thought she was the most beautiful woman in the world.

No more. What love he had felt for her had faded with her betrayal years ago.

"Good evening, Mother."

He shut the door behind him. What he had to say was private, and he did not want anyone to know she was here.

She rose from the chair like a queen. With the glass of brandy in her hand, she strode to him, her arms outstretched in welcome.

"Vincent. It is you. For a moment, I thought I might be dreaming. I cannot believe how much you look like your father."

He moved away before she could embrace him. "My father is dead, madam. If you encounter him, you have likely found your way to the Netherworld instead of my drawing room."

She took a sip of her brandy. "Still angry, I see."

"Anger is all I have left for you."

Frost walked over to the table where Sparrow had placed a crystal decanter of brandy and several glasses. *God bless the man,* he thought grimly. The butler knew his lord would need more than one glass of brandy to get through this visit. He removed the stopper and poured himself a generous glass. The first sip made him wince.

He had forgotten about the cut at the corner of his mouth.

"Were you in a fight?" she asked, noticing his reaction.

"Concerned? Don't bother. It was not much of one. Most of my opponents underestimate me." He deliberately picked the oversize chair his mother had recently relinquished. "I have a bad habit of fighting dirty."

His mother laughed. "Well, son, I had wondered if there was some part of me in you."

"Only the worst, I fear."

She sobered at his cutting remark. "I see your father in you as well."

"Please. Speaking ill of the dead is beneath you. You'll have to come up with something better to get under my skin, Mother." He sat back in his chair, his relaxed pose giving nothing away that he did not want her to see. "Now that we have gotten the pleasantries out of the way, let's get down to business. What do you want?"

"Is it wrong for a mother to visit her only son?" she complained, turning away as if he had hurt her with his coldness.

"Am I your only son? During your long absence, I assumed you might have produced a bastard or two with one of your lovers. Not that it is my concern."

"The only bastard I see is you."

Frost merely grinned and wagged his finger at her. "Careful. You want something from me, remember? Give me one reason why I shouldn't have my butler escort you out of my house."

His mother finished her brandy and laid the glass on the table in front of him. "I want to see my daughter," she said bluntly.

The hand on the armrest curled over the carved wood. "No."

"No?" she echoed in disbelief. "That is all you have to say on the subject? Just, no?"

"We have an agreement, you and I."

"I have not forgotten our agreement, Vincent. The annual payments that I receive from your solicitor arrive on time and you have been generous, but I—"

Frost could not believe her audacity. "Do you recall your part in our little arrangement, Mother? I make those payments to keep you away from Regan."

"She's my daughter!"

"You relinquished your rights when you abandoned your children." At her pained expression, he said, "That's right. You expected your fourteen-year-old son to raise your daughter. I had Father's friends to advise me on financial matters, but the servants helped me look after my eight-year-old sister. We managed without you, and will continue to do so once you find another protector to warm your bed."

His mother edged toward him. He admired her courage.

"You don't understand. When they told me that your father had died in a hunting accident—"

"Spare me, madam. My father had been dead five years when you decided to run off with your married lover after he killed his opponent in a botched duel and was obliged to leave the country. Pray, do not claim to be the grieving widow. You were never discreet when some gent asked you to shed your widow weeds."

She picked up the decanter of brandy and refilled his glass. "I hurt you. I know I made mistakes."

"I no longer care. What I do care about is Regan. She believes you're dead, you know. My sister cried for you, and then she began to forget all about you. The bit of irony is that you had yet to flee your burdensome life."

"How long do you intend to punish me?"

Frost had been wrong about his initial assessment when he entered the room. His mother looked tired and old. He wagered that her last lover had used up her funds and left her for a younger wench.

"Do you truly want Regan to learn that your married lover was more important to you than your children? That you turned your back on us without a pang of remorse? Hell, even I thought you had perished at sea until I received your first letter six years ago." His upper lip curled as he leaned forward. "I paid your blackmail to spare Regan. Her feelings are my only concern. She thinks you're in a grave. Do me the courtesy of staying there!"

He tossed back the contents of his glass, this time welcoming the stinging pain. "If it's money you're after . . . name your price. I can afford it."

"What if I want more than money, Vincent? What if I wish to stay?"

She knelt down beside him and tentatively reached out to caress his face. He grabbed her by the wrist and squeezed until she cried out in pain.

"A very unwise decision," he said, pulling her onto her feet. "Take the money before I withdraw my generous offer."

Her eyes welled with tears. "I heard that she is married and has a child. A son, I believe."

Who had told her? As far as he knew, his mother had severed all ties when she had left England. "Your sources speak the truth. If I hear that you have approached her or her family, I will make you sorely wish that you had drowned at sea."

"More threats, Vincent?" she asked wearily. "You were such a sweet-natured boy. The man that you have become breaks my heart."

"You will recover," he said drily.

She gave up the pretense of being wounded by his callous behavior. "I will require some time to consider your offer."

"Blackmail isn't an offer, madam. And proposing to pay you *more* is a bribe," he pointed out. "Do us both a favor and take it. Use it to attract another lover."

His mother dismissed the suggestion with a wave

of her hand. "I have returned to England for other reasons. I cannot leave until I have addressed them."

Short of tying her up and having Sparrow toss her off the nearest bridge into the Thames, he had to wait. "Fine. Deal with your business, but stay away from my family."

She gave him a disgruntled look. "I am family, Vincent."

"Not any longer." He escorted her to the door and rang for his butler. "And my name is Frost."

Chapter Ten

A few days later, Emily was sitting in the breakfast room silently debating her next step with Lord Chillingsworth. Should she reveal her hand and confront him about Lucy or avoid him?

Keeping her distance might prove difficult, she conceded. Regan had already extended an invitation to call on her. She wanted to show off her son and introduce her to her friends.

"Perhaps Lord Pashley has a brother," her mother had remarked when she had mentioned Regan's invitation.

According to her, the investment in Miss Swann's school had been worth every penny.

Emily deliberately failed to point out that her friend had an unmarried brother. She did not wish to encourage her mother.

"What is L-O-V?" her sister Judith inquired as she peered over Emily's shoulder.

Exasperated, she brushed away the toast crumbs her younger sister dropped. "Nothing," she said curtly, turning the paper over. She had been reluctant to spell out Lords of Vice, but she had marked them down since they were connected to Lord Chillingsworth.

"L-O-V . . . Simple enough to deduce. Emily was spelling *love* but she had forgotten the *E,*" Cedric chimed in from across the table.

"I was not spelling *love,* you twit," Emily said, grinding her molars together at his knowing grin. "I was spelling . . ."

She could not think of a single word!

"What is going on?" her mother asked, lifting her gaze from the paper. She had the uncanny ability to ignore all of them when she concentrated hard enough.

"Emily is in love," Cedric teased.

She huffed. "Do not listen to Cedric, Mother. I am not in love."

"L-O-V-E," he said, shoving his mouth full of eggs.

"Well, in fairness, Emily did forget the *E,*" her sister reminded her twin. "Maybe she was simply contemplating the notion of love."

"I did not forget—oh, for heaven's sake!" Emily gave up. "The twins are both wrong. I was dabbling in some poetry."

"Because she is in—"

There was a quiet knock at the door. Emily slapped her hand on the table in frustration as she stood. "Do not finish that sentence."

"Or what?"

She walked around the table, pausing long enough

to smack him on the top of the head. "I will quietly murder you if you do."

Cedric rubbed his head. "That makes no sense. If you are planning to murder me, I doubt I will be quiet about it."

Emily ignored him. The door opened before she could reach for the knob.

"You startled me, Miss Emily. I came to tell you that there is a gentleman in the front hall."

"Well, what does he want?"

"To see you."

"Are you positive?" Judith asked. "Perhaps he's here to see me."

"No one wants to see you if you persist in chewing with your mouth full, my dear," her mother said, signaling for the footman to remove her daughter's plate. "Did the gentleman give you his card?"

"Yes, madam. Here it is."

The butler handed it to Emily. She read the name and clapped her hand over her mouth to muffle her gasp.

"Who is it?" her mother asked, her attention on the paper again.

"Uh, no one you know." Emily crumbled the card in her hand. "I believe the gentleman has called on our residence by mistake. No need to get up. I will take care of it."

She dashed out of the breakfast room.

Cedric glanced at his twin sister. "Emily has forgotten more than an *E* this morning. She has lost her wits."

"Love will do that to a girl," Judith said, stealing her sister's untouched plate of food.

Frost straightened and smiled the moment Emily entered the room. The lady did not appear to be pleased to see him. Her hesitation at the threshold had him wondering if she might flee. However, he already knew she was made of sterner stuff.

"Why, Emily, don't you look lovely," he said, devouring her with his gaze.

She wore a long-sleeved apple-green morning dress with a white muslin pelerine that was secured with a gold pin just above her breasts. Most of her red hair was stuffed under a plain white crepe cap that was trimmed with satin, the color matching her dress.

Emily Cavell looked so prim and proper. He suddenly wanted to tug off her cap and kiss her senseless. He moved to greet her properly.

She curtsied and extended her hand. "How did you find me?" she whispered.

Frost bowed, his lips lightly brushing her bare knuckles. "It wasn't that difficult. Your father is well-known in town." He pulled her closer. "Is there a reason why we are whispering?" he asked, releasing her hand.

Emily cleared her throat. "Has something happened to Katie?" She glanced over her shoulder as if she was worried about someone overhearing their conversation.

Frost frowned. "Not at all. I told you that Katie is well and thriving in her new home."

"Then why have you come?"

It was hardly the enthusiastic welcome he had been hoping for, but her prickly nature challenged and amused him. Most ladies adored him. He could not fathom why she resisted the attraction between them. It was there in her hazel eyes as she silently debated whether he was a saint or the devil. He tasted it on her lips. It floated on the air around them.

He was a man who embraced his baser instincts. Emily Cavell could learn a thing or two from him.

"Did you not get my sister's invitation?"

Her forehead furrowed with confusion. "She sent a note, inviting me to visit and meet her son. However, we have yet to set a date."

It was unusual for his sister to forget such an important detail, but he had been the one who had encouraged her to send the note to Emily. Frost had wanted to see her again. The gathering would also give her a chance to meet his friends. If he could not persuade her to give up her crusade to shut down Nox, perhaps one of the others could.

"Regan seems to think otherwise." He slipped his arm through hers and led her to the door. "Don't fret, my dear, it's just a small gathering of family. And I volunteered to be your escort. Are you ready to depart or do you wish to change your dress?"

Emily withdrew her arm and moved away from him. He could sense that she was torn. She did not want to disappoint Regan, but she was not willing to place herself into his hands.

A pity since he could bring a woman to completion with his fingers alone, but such a declaration would send her fleeing to the safety of her bedchamber.

He would have to be patient, and that was difficult when he saw something he wanted—and he wanted Emily.

"And who is this?"

Frost had been so distracted by the woman standing next to him that he had not noticed her mother's approach. Emily appeared to be startled by her presence.

He bowed. "Good afternoon, madam. I am Vincent Bishop, Earl of Chillingsworth."

The lady brightened at his name. "It is a pleasure, Lord Chillingsworth. Are you here for Emily? She said when she saw your card that you had called on the wrong residence."

Frost cast an amused look at Emily. "It is no mistake, Mrs. Cavell. My sister, Lady Pashley, asked me to drive your daughter to the small gathering that she is having." He paused, his face clouding with concern. "Though there seems to be some confusion on the date."

"Confusion? Nonsense." Her mother's mouth thinned with exasperation. She had more experience in dealing with her stubborn daughter, and Frost was happy to accept her assistance. "Emily, if Lady Pashley is expecting you and has generously provided you a handsome escort, then you must accept."

"Mother, I was about to—"

"Ah, no arguments," she said, taking Emily by the arm and directing her toward the stairs. "Wash your face and change your dress. I will keep your

Lord Chillingsworth company while he waits for your return."

"Lord Chillingsworth isn't *my* anything," she grumbled, but she dutifully headed for the stairs.

Satisfied with his victory, Frost crossed his hands behind his back and followed Mrs. Cavell into the parlor.

Chapter Eleven

"Do I owe you an apology?" Emily asked thirty minutes later after she and Lord Chillingsworth had bid farewell to her mother. With her maid's assistance, she had hastily changed exchanged her morning dress for a striped yellow jaconet muslin dress with a corded band around the waist and a scalloped flounce at the bottom. There was nothing she could do with her hair but pin it up. She covered it with a large, flat-brimmed leghorn hat trimmed with a yellow satin ribbon and bow.

He squinted at her as he adjusted the reins in his hands. "Why do you presume that one is necessary?"

Emily could not fathom why he sounded so amused.

"I abandoned you to the tender mercies of my mother," she replied, hoping her answer would suffice.

It was her mother's fault that she was sitting beside him in his phaeton. While she recoiled at the thought of disappointing Regan, Emily was reluctant to spend any time alone with the earl as she struggled with the notion that he could very well be Lucy's seducer.

How can you be certain if you do not confront him?

Her sleep had been restless as dreams of Lucy dying in her arms, and Frost's kisses, pulled her into two different directions. The problem was that a part of her actually liked the arrogant gentleman. He had proven to be brave and protective, and he had managed to make her laugh. She had no doubts that he had lived up to his reputation as a Lord of Vice. However, was he capable of seducing a young innocent who had been betrothed to another gentleman? Could he be so calculating and cruel?

What if she accused him, and the charges proved false? Not only would Lord Chillingsworth sever all ties to her, she could possibly ruin her friendship with Regan. Then there were her mother's high hopes that she might find a respectable gentleman to court her during their stay in London. The earl and his friends could cause trouble in that regard. An unkind word in the right gossip's ear and the doors of the *ton* would be closed to her family. It would matter little that her mother was Lord Ketchen's youngest daughter. The family had neither the wealth nor the influence to declare war on the earl.

"Not exactly a chatterbox, are you?" the man who called himself Frost said, interrupting her thoughts. "A very admirable trait in a lady. It makes the drive quite pleasant. Is this something you learned while you resided at Miss Swann's Academy for Young Ladies?"

She tilted her head to glance at him. "Why do you ask?"

"I'm tempted to ask for a refund. None of the Miss Swann's lessons seemed to make an adequate impression on my sister," he explained, sounding disgruntled. "The school was supposed to instruct her on how to be a lady, and what I received was a disrespectful brat."

Emily laughed at his description of Regan. "For a brat, your sister has managed quite well. She married Lord Pashley and presented him with a son. Unless it is a love match, most married couples would be content."

He only offered her his profile, but she noticed his right brow arch at her comment. "Just content? I would have never guessed that you were cynical about marriage. However, to answer your unspoken question, yes, my sister and that bounder husband of hers love each other. I would have had to kill Dare to keep him away from Regan."

He handled the reins and horses skillfully as they rounded another corner. When she realized they were entering Hyde Park, she asked, "Why have you brought me here? I thought your sister was expecting us?' "

"Are you accusing me of lying, Miss Cavell?" He made a soft chiding sound.

"No!"

He chuckled at her bald-faced lie. "Well, Regan is expecting us. However, I took the liberty of collecting you early."

"Why?"

He gestured at the landscape. "I thought a drive through the park would please you. It is still early for the fashionable to be parading about, but it will give us the opportunity to finish our discussion."

Emily nibbled at her lip. The earl was referring to what they had been doing before Regan and her husband's timely arrival. "There is little to address," she said lightly. "If I recall, I was about to leave and join my family when your sister came upon us."

"While we were kissing," he said bluntly.

No amount of will could prevent her skin from heating in embarrassment at the reminder. With any luck, Lord Chillingsworth would believe she was getting too much sun.

"We had already finished."

The corners of his mouth curved into a knowing smile. "I was not quite finished. I was just giving you a moment to recover."

Such arrogance! "You did not overwhelm me with a kiss, my lord. I was"—she struggled for a glib retort—"bored."

The earl indelicately snorted. "You were not bored."

Warming up to her topic, she shifted so her knees pressed against his leg. "Of course, I was surprised. I barely know you, Lord Chillingsworth."

"Frost," he said tersely.

She was not quite prepared to address him by that name. "Yes, *frost* aptly describes the kiss," she said, deliberately misunderstanding. "Brittle, chilly, and I was reluctant to linger."

She braced for his reaction. Had she gone too far? Having two brothers, she knew a blow to a man's pride was capable of creating unanticipated consequences.

Lord Chillingsworth muttered something unintelligible under his breath as he slowed the horses. His right arm snaked around her waist and hauled her close. "The devil you say!"

Her hat was knocked askew as his mouth closed over hers. While the kiss was forceful, he reminded her that there was nothing brittle or chilly about his lips. They were unexpectedly soft against hers. He tasted divine, she thought with a sigh as she returned his kiss.

Lord Chillingsworth—no—Frost gave her lower lip a nip before he pulled away. "You look overly warm, Miss Cavell. You might want to fix your hat to keep the sun from browning your fair skin."

He grinned at her bemused expression as he adjusted the reins, directing the horses back onto the gravel road.

Emily glanced around to see if anyone had noticed. "What if someone had seen us?" she asked, relieved for the moment that they were alone.

"It's doubtful. It's too early for the gossips, and anyone else is of little consequence," he said dismissively.

Her hands were shaking when she reached up to adjust the angle of her hat. "I did not give you permission to kiss me, Lord Chillingsworth."

"I have kissed you twice, Emily. The intimacy grants you the right to use the name my family and friends use." He gave her a speculative glance. "No one will think you're shameless if you do."

"Perhaps not," she said, retying the satin strings on her hat. "Even so, I highly doubt being in your company is good for my reputation."

"I disagree."

Naturally, he would. Frost was not the one who had to worry about his conduct. "So the gossips are spinning lies to amuse the *ton*?"

His cheeks became more pronounced as he contemplated her question. "It depends."

"On what precisely?"

"Which stories you've heard," he countered.

What about the rumors of you seducing young innocents for sport?

Emily could not bring herself to ask the question out loud. Instead, she lowered her gaze and focused on his gloved hand, which rested idly on his thigh. She recalled the strength and warmth of it as he pulled her against him.

"Should we be concerned about the time?" she said, slightly breathless at the realization that she wanted him to kiss her again. "It would be rude to arrive late."

"My sister is used to my rudeness."

She flinched when he expectantly reached up to brush aside a yellow satin string that had become caught on one of the buttons on her bodice.

"Thank you."

"My pleasure," he replied, aware that he was making her nervous. "Rudeness. Some consider it a character flaw, but I have found it useful."

"And what does the person who must suffer your rudeness tell you?"

"Oh, they probably think I am an arse," he said, signaling the horses to move off their gravel course and onto the grass. "Though most don't have the courage to say it."

"Why are we stopping?" Emily wondered if he was planning to kiss her again. "What about your sister?"

With the phaeton halted, she felt the impact of his turquoise-blue gaze. "Forget about Regan. I want to talk about why you are so interested in bringing down Nox."

Chapter Twelve

"Nox?" she echoed. How had they gone from kissing to discussing the gentlemen's club? Then she recalled that Regan had mentioned the club belonged to the Lords of Vice. "I have not patronized the establishment."

He absently rubbed his face. "Not unexpected, since the club is strictly for males. Women have been known to visit the gambling hell. However, they are not the kind who fret about their reputations."

He was speaking of prostitutes, poor lost creatures who were willing to sell their bodies for a few coins and a fleeting pleasure that never quite made them whole again.

She gave him a level look. "Then I consider myself fortunate to be burdened with morals and common sense. I have no desire to patronize such a place."

His beautiful mouth twitched. "Truly? You aren't a bit curious?"

"Not at all!" she huffed in outrage.

"Aw, come now, Emily," he said silkily. "You must have a notion about what takes place in such an establishment. After all, rumor has it that if you had your way you would rid London of all its corruption and vices."

She grew still at his revelation. People had been gossiping about *her*? The notion was absurd. "Who told you that?"

"It isn't important," he said dismissively. "What concerns me is your interest in Nox. While your little moral crusade amuses me, it is also very dangerous."

"Are you threatening me, Lord Chillingsworth?" she asked in hushed tones. A small part of her was hopeful that he was, since it would settle her internal debate about his character.

"And confirm your worst suspicions about me or Nox?" He grunted. "Hardly. No, little innocent, Nox is nothing to concern yourself with."

"What about you?"

"Oh, you should worry about me, Emily," he said softly. "But that is neither here nor there. The danger of which I speak of is that of the genuine criminals in this town. There are numerous unpleasant individuals who would gladly slit your throat if you prevent them from turning a profit on their various criminal enterprises."

"And what of Nox? You do not consider it illegal and corrupt?"

"You would have to be more specific, and I doubt you would be pleased with my answers. What you should be aware of is that the club belongs to the Lords of Vice, my dear. You might want to remember that when you are surrounded by the seven founding members at my sister's house."

Regan had invited everyone to her house this afternoon. It was a disconcerting thought. She had assumed that Frost had been invited because he was family. "And what if I ignore your sage advice?"

"Oh, I would not recommend it, Emily." He moistened his lips, and the look he gave her weakened her knees. It was a good thing that she was already sitting. "Besides, I can be quite persuasive when I want something."

"And what do you want, Lord Chillingsworth?"

"For you to leave Nox alone," he said flatly. His turquoise-blue eyes softened and warmed at the distress that she could not conceal. "And other things, but they are best put aside for now."

The earl reached for the reins he had secured. "Perhaps you are correct. As pleasant as this drive has been, we should continue on to my sister's residence."

He turned the phaeton about, heading for the entrance of the park.

Emily nodded, marveling that Lord Chillingsworth could deliver kisses and threats with jaunty aplomb. It was obvious that he could be ruthless when the situation required. Nox meant something to him, and it was a vulnerability she could exploit if she was brave enough.

Or foolish enough.

The earl could be a deadly foe.

"So why Nox?" he asked, though she was not fooled by his casual tone.

"I beg your pardon?"

He smiled humorlessly. "Do not be coy, Emily. Why has Nox caught your interest?"

She wrinkled her nose. "I never said that I was curious about your club," she replied with honesty. She had been unaware of Lord Chillingsworth's connection to Nox when she expressed her frustration that evening to the group of ladies. "If you are listening to gossip, you have to concede that truth is often in short supply."

"So indulge my curiosity. Why is a beautiful lady dabbling in such risky amusements?"

Although he was not glancing in her direction, she could not resist shrugging. "With my father and soon my brother immersed in the law, the subjects of crime and injustices have often been debated at our family table."

"So you are a bluestocking?" He shook his head, his handsome face contemplative as he attempted to figure out her motives. "No, that is not enough."

"You are referring to several conversations, my lord, that you were not even around to witness," she said, not bothering to hide her frustration. "You credit me with too much ambition."

"I disagree." He spared her a quick glance. "Lest you forget, I was present for your confrontation with Katie's stepfather."

She scowled but did not contradict him.

"You have plenty of ambition, Emily. Heart and courage, too. I want to understand why this business about the clubs is so personal for you."

Emily did not immediately reply, silently debating whether she should tell him the truth. Finally, she said, "It involves my sister."

"The younger one who has a twin?" He answered

his own question before she could reply. "No, it must be the older one. The one who died."

"Yes," she said, treading carefully around the uncomfortable subject.

His brow furrowed. "Forgive me for being indelicate, but I see no way to avoid it. Does your sister's death have anything to do with why the crimes on King Street and the surrounding area have upset you?"

"No. Why would you assume that?" The wrenching painful twist that she felt in her chest was a familiar companion whenever Lucy was mentioned. "My sister took her own life," Emily said dully. "The details are not known outside my family, so if I hear any gossip I'll know its source."

"Are you threatening me, my dear?" he teased, echoing her earlier question.

She did not have to think about it. "Yes," she said a bit too sweetly.

Frost tipped back his head and laughed. "Just another reason why you intrigue me, Emily."

"I cannot fathom why," she muttered. It would be best if he stayed away from her.

"Seeking compliments?" he asked, his voice stroking her like silk. "Come closer, and I shall whisper them in your ear."

"No, thank you," she said crisply, using the ice in her voice to conceal her delicate shudder at the thought of his mouth and breath so close to her ear.

"We'll save that for another time." He sighed. "So you lost your sister. You have my sympathies. Though, if you want my opinion, your sister was a selfish chit for hurting the very people who obviously cherished her."

Emily sucked in her breath. Over the years, as she had watched her mother and father grieve the loss of their daughter, the same traitorous thought about her sister's selfishness had crept into her head. "You, of all people, have no right to mock my grief or my sister's death."

"My darling girl, I am not mocking anyone," he countered, sounding slightly peeved. He explained, "Life is to be celebrated and treasured, and while your loss is tragic, it is even more so since your sister's foolishness is contagious."

Emily gaped at him in astonishment. "Contagious? Were you not listening? My sister did not die of a disease."

It was her spirit that had wasted away.

He flashed an impatient glance in her direction. "I am referring to this nonsense of you challenging criminals and club owners because you do not approve of how they go about their business."

"I haven't done anything," she protested. If he persisted in beleaguering her about his beloved Nox, she might be tempted to do something that would truly upset him.

"Nothing too troubling," he amended in a futile attempt to calm her down. "Yet. But you cannot dismiss that you have sown a few seeds of dissent within certain circles."

"Good heavens, you are behaving as if I wield influence over these ladies. Though it is no business of yours, I only participated in several conversations on the rising crime in London. All I am guilty of is offering my opinion."

As they drew nearer to the entrance of the park, Emily noted that the number of carriages and pedestrians had increased. She had been so distracted by her argument with Frost that she had not noticed they were no longer alone.

It was then that she observed a gentleman on horseback approaching from the opposite direction. She brought her hand up to shield her eyes from the sunlight. Emily had been in such a rush to whisk the earl out of the house that she had forgotten to bring her parasol. The blond-haired gentleman was impeccably dressed, and his looks were passable. She might have given him only a passing glance if she did not recognize him.

"Miss Cavell," he said politely, touching the brim of his hat out of respect as his gaze shifted to Lord Chillingsworth. "Always a pleasure to see you again. London life suits you."

The man did not alter his casual pace, nor did her companion slow down the phaeton.

"Why, thank you"—oh, bother, what was the man's name?—"uh, Mr. Hal—"

"Halward," Frost said though clenched teeth.

The earl did not acknowledge the man in any other way. If there was history between the two, neither intended to mention it in her presence.

His horse and their carriage passed by each other, and Emily had to look over her shoulder to see the man's reaction. She caught a glimpse of the slight smirk on Mr. Halward's face before he turned away and continued down the road.

Frost literally vibrated with suppressed fury. "You have chosen a very perilous path, Miss Cavell. One that I order you to reconsider," he said grimly.

Emily did not understand why he was so upset with her. Nevertheless, she did not appreciate his bossy tone. "You are not in a position to order me about, Lord Chillingsworth!"

His thunderous expression had her shrinking away from him. "Press me, and you will find out what I am capable of doing when I am provoked."

Emily wisely decided not to say another word until they reached Lord and Lady Pashley's residence.

Chapter Thirteen

Regan hurried from the garden terrace cuddling her tired son when she heard her brother's voice from within the house. "Frost has arrived with Miss Cavell," she announced, turning away from the open doors and approaching her husband, Vane, and Sin, who had been quietly debating politics around a nearby table.

"Are you planning to scold him for being late?" Dare asked.

Regan rolled her eyes. "There isn't much point. He is always late."

Often she wondered if he was putting up with the lot of them. If she pressed him too hard, she feared that he would stop coming at all.

"Well, he might have a good reason," Sin said distractedly as he watched his gleeful wife give Reign's croquet ball a good wallop and sent it rolling across the lawn. Saint, Hunter, Grace, and Sophia applauded. Reign, noticing his friend's regard, gestured for him to do something about Juliana.

Unsympathetic, Sin shrugged. Reign was probably losing. Again.

"I hope so," Dare replied, sounding amused. "It was the reason why I asked Regan to give him the task."

Understanding lit Vane's gaze. "So she is beautiful?"

"Stunning." Dare said, giving his wife a sheepish grin when she frowned at him. "And a redhead. Though from the look of things the other night at the Fiddicks' ball, Frost is already captivated by the lady."

Regan's frown deepened at the news. "Emily is a friend. I will not have Frost seducing her just because he has a fondness for redheads. I expect all of you to make certain he behaves himself."

She did not bother to wait for a reply from her husband and their friends. All of them loved her brother as much as she did. Rubbing her son's back, she tilted her head and noted that he was almost asleep. She slowly moved toward the open door.

They had a full house this afternoon. Juliana and Reign were playing a boisterous game of croquet, while Catherine, Isabel, and Dare's fifteen-year-old niece were walking the garden paths.

It was not until she stepped into the library that she heard the angry voices downstairs. Who the devil was Frost shouting at? Her housekeeper appeared in the doorway, and she looked as worried as Regan.

"Madam, we have a small problem," the older woman began.

"I will take care of it," Regan assured her. "Could you take Bishop upstairs? He just fell asleep."

She handed her son to the housekeeper. *Thank you,* she mouthed, and headed toward the stairs to see what all the commotion was all about.

"Come with me."

A soft gasp escaped Emily's lips when Frost took her hand and led her upstairs instead of following the housekeeper to one of the doors that would have taken them outdoors.

"Where are we going?" she said, slightly breathless as she was forced to keep up with his long stride. "Your sister is outdoors with—"

"My sister will wait. You and I have a few things to discuss, and I prefer to keep our chat private."

"Is this about Nox?" she asked, trying to understand what was driving his temper. "I told you everything that—"

"Forget about Nox for a moment," he snapped, striding by what she deduced was the Pashleys' drawing room.

Likely a frequent guest in his sister's residence, he navigated the maze of passageways as if it were his own. He halted in front of a closed door, opened it, and peeked inside. Satisfied that it was empty, he stepped in. "Come." With his hand firmly entwined with his, she followed.

It was a small anteroom that with a narrow arched window at the end. Four heavy benches covered with dark blue and gold silk were positioned along the wall. Above, Etruscan vases of various sizes were on display.

"No one should bother us," he offered as an

explanation on why he had selected this particular room.

"Fine," Emily said with a delicate toss of her head. Free to roam the narrow confines of the room, she walked over to one of the cushioned benches and sat down. "Ask your questions."

"Halward," he said succinctly. "How are you acquainted with the man?"

"Why?"

"Indulge me," he said, taking the seat opposite her.

She saw no reason not to humor him. "I have met him twice. The first time was in the drawing room of a Mr. Reid. He is an acquaintance of my father."

"And the second time?" he impatiently prompted.

"At the Leicester Square Rotunda. My mother wished to view the panorama. Why?" she asked, puzzled by his anger and concern.

He braced his elbows on his knees as he leaned forward. "Do not be fooled by his civility, Emily. Halward is no gentleman."

Her eyes glittered with amusement. "The same might be said about you, Lord Chillingsworth."

"Pay attention," he snapped, his face darkening with anger. "The man has the means to mingle with the fringes of polite society, but he is not one of us. His connections extend to the lowest criminals London has to offer. I am astounded your father would place his daughter in the presence of such a man."

Emily barely knew the man, so she could not defend against Frost's accusations. "It was not my father's fault that Mr. Halward happened to be attending the same function—or that later, we saw him again at the rotunda. Mere coincidences. Besides, the man said nothing untoward to me or my family. If anyone has been arrogant, rude, and overstepped his bounds, it is you."

She rose from the bench.

"If that is all, I would like to greet my host and hostess."

Frost also stood, his turquoise-blue eyes lingering on her face. "Not quite. I want you to promise me that you will stay away from Halward."

"Another order, my lord?" she said softly. "Your threats and orders are getting tiresome."

He grinned down at her, reminding her of a hungry wolf. "Defy me, and I promise—"

"What?" she interrupted, not really intimidated by him. "You have no power over me."

Emily turned away, intending to join the other guests outdoors, but the earl had other plans. This time she was prepared for his kiss. Her mouth parted as his slanted over it. Frost tugged her closer until her bodice pressed against his chest. She daringly rested her hands against the front of his frock coat, and felt the solid muscle of his chest. His body was as firm as his high-handed dictates, she thought, as his tongue teased hers.

Emily was taken aback by her own body's responses. Her nipples had tightened, and she longed to rub away the sensation. She felt her heart pounding in her chest, and a rousing heat coursed through her body. Impulsively she leaned against him, savoring the feel of him. Frost had placed one hand on her arm and the other on her hip as he worked his magic with his talented mouth. He was silently demanding something from her, and a part of her was willing to grant him anything.

The realization was the splash of cold water that she desperately required. While Frost railed at her about the dangers surrounding her, he might prove the biggest one of all.

Emily pushed him away, ignoring the regret she felt and cursing her weakness.

"You are very persuasive, Lord Chillingsworth," she said, unable to keep her voice level. He unsettled her in so many ways. "However, I believe we are finished with today's lesson."

Emily walked out of the room and was startled to find Regan waiting for her in the passageway. Was she aware of her indiscreet activities with Frost? Of course she was. All she had to do was take one look at her flushed features and reddened lips. She braced herself for questions. However, Regan was a better friend than that.

"I have a room where you may fix your hair and compose yourself," her friend said, her gaze flickering to the empty doorway as if she expected her brother to appear. "When you are ready, I'll introduce you to the rest of the family."

Emily nodded, wondering how long she could avoid facing Frost again.

"Why is Regan vexed with you?" Dare asked several hours later when he managed to catch Frost alone.

"Is she vexed?" was his innocent reply. "I hadn't noticed."

"There has to be some reason she has been glaring at you all afternoon," his brother-in-law said, unperturbed that his wife had been barely civil to her brother.

"Another hint was the smack on the back of your head she delivered when she walked by you," Hunter added, overhearing Dare's comment. "I haven't seen Regan this angry since the day you suggested that my plan to whisk Grace to Gretna Green would go smoother if I poured laudanum into her wine."

Aye, it had taken his sister a few weeks to recover from Hunter and Grace's elopement. They had succeeded in the getting the couple married, but she had not approved of the duke's high-handed scheme.

"If I recall, Regan was angry with you, not me," Frost argued. "You had made a mess of things with your bride-to-be. I was just being helpful."

His friends exchanged glances. They had both been on the receiving end of Frost's help, and learned there was always a price.

"Just be grateful that Grace eventually forgave me," Hunter muttered as his gaze sought out his duchess.

Frost observed that Grace was engaged in what appeared to be a serious conversation with Reign and Sophia's daughter, Lily Grace, who was inordinately pleased to share a name with the Duchess of Huntsley. No one pointed out that she had been named years before Hunter had claimed his bride, and Grace was delighted by the young girl's adoration.

"Your duchess gave you your heir," Frost said. "When are you planning to give her a daughter?"

Hunter looked incredulous. "Our son is two months old, Frost. Necessity might have forced me to rush her into marriage and to produce an heir," he went on, his eyes clouding with guilt. "However, I can afford to be patient."

Frost nodded at the giggling child who was preening with Grace's bonnet on her head. "Look at them. Your duchess doesn't seem to mind her fate, gent."

If Hunter had a whit of sense, he would steal his wife away from the gathering and start working on the daughter that she obviously longed for.

"Hunter may be easy to distract, but I'm not," Dare interjected. "What is going on between you and Emily Cavell?"

"Nothing."

At least not at the moment.

Dare's eyes widened in growing wonder. "It's worse than I thought."

Frost did not have to feign his bewilderment. "How so?"

Hunter slowly nodded. "You're correct, Dare. How long has this been going on?"

Both gentlemen were daft. "I have no idea what you are babbling about."

"Hmm . . . defensive," Hunter noted. "And he's clearly lying. Another sign."

Frost privately conceded that he might deserve their teasing—he had enjoyed tormenting them as they struggled to win their ladies' hearts. Even so, his generosity was not infinite.

"I picked up Miss Cavell from her residence at

Regan's request," he said tersely. "Everything else is solely conjecture on your part."

"Regan and I caught them kissing at the Fiddicks' ball," Dare tattled. "He also chased off some young rakehells that were bothering the lady."

"Amorous and protective," Hunter said, speaking in a serious tone suggesting that Frost's actions held some hidden meaning. "Have you declared your intentions to Miss Cavell's family?"

Something close to panic churned in his gut. "What? Are you both mad? I have no desire to marry Emily Cavell or any lady. Sin had mentioned Miss Cavell's hatred for Nox, and I thought it best to keep an eye on her."

Dare rubbed at his nose. "Need I remind you that your interest in the lady was evident?" He deliberately glanced down at the front of Frost's trousers.

Hunter laughed. "How did I miss this?"

"You haven't missed anything." So what if kissing Emily Cavell had hardened his cock? He was a man in his prime. He would have had the same reaction with any woman. "I was restless and sought to amuse myself with the lady."

"Which is precisely why Regan is furious with you," Dare said, speaking to him as if he were thick-witted. "Nox has been denounced in the past by the *ton,* and our doors remained open. I would not trouble yourself with one lady's disapproval. Miss Cavell is harmless."

Frost disagreed. Emily was breaking down his control and peace of mind. Earlier, when he had been kissing her in the anteroom, and had wondered how far he could have pushed her, he had longed to tug on her bodice until he gained access to her breasts. Would she have cradled his head, allowing him to cup those generous mounds and suck her nipples? Would she have protested if his hand had slipped under her skirt or would she have squirmed against his fingers, begging to be touched? If he had not heard Regan's approach, he might have sated his curiosity.

It was out of character for him not to share the details of affairs. However, Emily's friendship with Regan complicated matters for him. He had to tread carefully, or even his friends would dissuade him from his course.

"Halward has taken an interest in Miss Cavell," Frost exaggerated, though he sensed he was not straying too far from the truth. Nor did he believe it was a coincidence that Emily had encountered the man twice. "The man has not made any secret that he would like to take control of Nox, and I suspect he is not above using the lady to help in this endeavor. It serves our purposes to offer her protection, even if she is unaware of it."

It served his interests as well.

Emily was wary of him. With Regan's assistance, she had managed to avoid him, but he was content to let her sulk. He planned to end this nonsense when he offered to escort the lady back to her family. His sister might huff and protest, but she would not stand in his way. After all, she had been the one to ask him to collect her friend.

Neither he nor Emily was comfortable with the notion that they were attracted to each other. Frost was not troubled by lust. It was healthy, and expressing it was pleasurable while it lasted. Having Emily Cavell in his bed was something he craved as strongly as food. However, unlike his past lovers, the lady would expect and deserve more from him. Unfortunately, he knew he was incapable of satisfying her heart as thoroughly as her body.

Chapter Fourteen

"No need to trouble yourself, brat. I will see Emily home."

Frost had made the announcement to his sister hours before dusk could cast its shadow over London. He had brought her to the Pashleys' residence; logic dictated that he would be the one to bring her home.

Emily had felt Regan's questioning gaze on her, but she did not acknowledge it. Thankfully, her friend had not pressed her on what she had overheard within the narrow anteroom in her house. To her surprise, Emily had enjoyed the gathering.

As Frost had predicted, she had been introduced to the other Lords of Vice: Dare, Reign, Sin, Vane, Hunter, and Saint. It was obvious by the tales that had been shared and their unguarded affection for one another that the gentlemen had a long history of friendship and rivalry. With the exception of Frost, all of the gentlemen were married, and she could not fault their choices in wives. She liked every one of them, and all of them had done their part to make her feel welcome.

Of course, there were speculative glances among them as she and Frost circled each other. He was the sole bachelor of the group; it was natural his friends would wish to see him settled with a wife at his side.

If anyone had bothered to ask, Emily could have told them that she was not that lady. Or perhaps they already knew.

To prove that she was not afraid of him or the attraction that seemed to flare to life when he was close, Emily had stared into Frost's exotic turquoise-blue gaze and thanked him for offering to take her home. He appeared startled that she was not fighting him. In truth, she was equally surprised, but there was something alluring about flirting with the forbidden.

And Lord Chillingsworth was not the type of man any respectable lady would encourage.

It was a quiet drive home. Perhaps it was due to the long day filled with lively debate and conversation, but neither felt inclined to speak. Emily found the silence comforting. She smiled to herself, thinking that Frost hardly qualified as a restful companion. He challenged and annoyed her. He teased and made her laugh. Then she thought of Lucy, and what joy she felt faded into the shadows. She was flirting with a gentleman who might very well be her enemy and the reason why her sister took her own life.

I am stronger than Lucy.

The fierce thought shamed Emily. Her sister hadn't been weak. She had been beautiful and generous; she had wanted to be loved. She had trusted the wrong man and her spirit had been broken.

"Here we are. Safe and relatively untouched," Frost said with a trace of humor as he secured the reins and disembarked from the phaeton to see to the horses.

Emily waited in the carriage for him to finish his task. He walked around to the side and held out both hands. Unsteadily, she started to rise, but Frost took matters literally into his hands. Without permission, he grabbed her firmly by the waist and lifted her to ensure her skirt was not smudged by the wheel of the carriage. His strength was impressive. There were no visible signs of exertion on his face when her feet touched the ground.

"Thank you, my lord."

With a casual shrug, he said, "I'll seize on any excuse to put my hands on you."

He extended his arm to her.

If her mother or sister was watching, they would be distressed to see her arguing with the earl. To placate any observers, she placed her hand on his coat sleeve. "You cannot speak to me thus."

"Why do you persist in tempting me to prove you wrong?" Together they started up the front walk. "Or is it that you secretly desire my touch?"

"No," she exclaimed a little too vehemently. "Do you know what you are, Lord Chillingsworth?"

"You have figured me out?" he asked, sounding impressed. "Quick, clever, and utterly kissable when you are vexed—I might have to marry you, after all!"

Her stomach fluttered like a jar filled with moths.

She refused to allow him to unbalance her again. "You are spoiled. You call your sister a brat, but I believe the nickname aptly applies to you."

"Pet names for me, too?" he teased. "Next you will be begging for my kisses."

"You are so accustomed to ladies falling at your feet that you have little respect for them," she said, refusing to be dissuaded from speaking her mind before she lost her courage. "These silly creatures foolishly offer their heart and favors, while you . . . you—"

She was horribly embarrassed that she had worked herself up to such a state, she was on the verge of crying.

Frost halted, the teasing light in his blue gaze winking out as she grew increasingly agitated. "What do I do, Emily?" he asked quietly.

"You seduce them, and—and cast them aside. It is your nature. You leave them heartbroken, friendless, and lost. In a fit of despair, they . . ." Emily shook her head, reluctant to continue.

"No, finish it," he said, his expression shuttered. "What does this mysterious lady do?"

Emily brought her fist to her mouth and sobbed. "She kills herself when she learns that she is carrying her lover's child."

Frost nodded almost absently. "Your sister."

"Lucy." Emily sniffed, then realized she had forgotten to tuck a handkerchief away in her reticule. She blinked as Frost produced one from a hidden pocket. Accepting it, she murmured her thanks.

"My sister's name is Lucy. Good evening, Lord Chillingsworth."

"Wait!"

She halted and glanced back at him. His tense, angry expression was no encouragement to linger.

"Lucy Cavell. Your sister was Lucy Cavell."

"She has been dead five years, my lord. Has so much time passed that you have forgotten her name?" she asked. The sadness expanding in her chest was almost unbearable.

"Let me get this straight. You think I callously seduced and abandoned your sister?" He took several steps toward her. When she edged away, he laughed bitterly. "This is rich. Aye, I knew a Lucy Cavell. I have not seen her in years, and did not connect the lady with you."

And why should he? She looked nothing like Lucy.

She turned to leave.

"One more thing before you dash off," Frost called out, his words causing her to stop. "I was never Lucy's lover."

With her hands curled into fists, Emily squeezed her eyes shut so tightly she would likely suffer a headache from the abuse. She fought to keep her emotions bottled inside. If she let go, she feared she would start screaming.

She did not conceal her anger and unspoken hatred toward the gentleman who inspired feelings that would betray the memory of her sister. "You, Lord Chillingsworth, are a liar."

Frost stared at her as if she were a stranger. "If

you were a man, I would call you out and put a bullet in you for such an insult."

"Then it is a good thing that I am not a man," she said, shaken by the cold fury in his voice. "Because I would die knowing that I was able to return the favor."

"You have the wrong gent, Emily," he said when she tried to turn away.

Her instincts told her that he believed what he was saying. It only proved that she knew little about men.

"Did I mention that I was the one who found her? I was fifteen years old, and could do nothing to save her. She was dying, and no one heard my cries as the hem of my skirt soaked up her blood." Emily twisted the handkerchief in her hand. "She was out of her head from the blood loss, but she whispered to me about the baby, about her mistakes, and begged me not to make the same ones."

Emily wanted to slap him for the pity she saw on his face.

He shook his head. "You must have been terrified."

Emily did not want his sympathy. She wanted answers. "I asked her who betrayed her, and she uttered one final word. Can you guess what that word might be?"

"Are we playing a game, Emily?" he asked lightly.

"Lucy said one word. *Frost*," she spat. "Now tell me again of your innocence, Lord Chillingsworth?"

His face whitened in shock.

"I thought not."

Throwing his handkerchief to the ground, Emily straightened her shoulders and walked into the house.

The earl did not make the mistake of calling her back.

Frost bent down and retrieved the handkerchief Emily had discarded. Lucy Cavell. How had he forgotten about that silly chit? He rubbed his thumb over the linen. It was damp with Emily's tears. She believed he was the vilest scoundrel. A man capable of planting his seed in a woman and then casting her and their unborn child aside.

I asked her who betrayed her, and she uttered one final word. Can you guess what that word might be?

Emily was wrong. Frost was not the man who had betrayed her sister. He was furious. At himself and Emily. She had not connected him to her sister when he had initially introduced himself to her. That had happened later. When? He stood there in front of the Cavells' house and thought for a moment. The Fiddicks' ball. Regan had called him Frost, and Emily had escaped. He had assumed it was the kiss that had upset her. Now he knew better.

Christ's bones! Angrily, he stuffed the handkerchief into the pocket of his coat. Frost cast an impotent final glance at the Cavells' front door before he headed for his carriage. Even if he pounded on the door and demanded to speak to Emily, she would not listen to him.

She believed him to be an immoral liar, a charming seducer, and a calculating scoundrel.

And the uncomfortable realization was—Emily was right.

He was guilty of being all three.

Emily sagged against the other side of the door as her tears left tracks on her cheeks. It hadn't been a mistake.

Five years ago, Frost had met Lucy in London.

He had seduced and discarded her as he probably had countless other women. Hadn't his own sister warned her to stay away from Frost? Of course, he had denied being her sister's lover. He also had appeared genuinely surprised about the news of Lucy's pregnancy. Nevertheless, it did not prove his innocence.

She assumed her sister intended to take the secret to her grave, but she had not counted on Emily discovering her. Confused and in pain, she had whispered the unthinkable into Emily's ear, never considering that her sister might seek out the gentleman who had ruined her.

"Emily, is that you?" Her mother's voice floated down from upstairs.

"Yes. I will be right there, Mother."

Hurriedly, she used the cuff of her sleeve to wipe away the evidence of her crying. She grimaced, wishing she hadn't tossed away Frost's handkerchief. Untying the yellow satin strings under her chin, she took her time as she climbed the stairs, taking a moment to compose herself.

When she reached the door to the drawing room, she gave her face a final swipe and pasted a smile on her face before she entered the room.

"Oh, Emily, dear," her mother said, not glancing up from her embroidery. "How was your afternoon with Lord and Lady Pashley?"

She removed her hat and smoothed her hair. "I had a wonderful time, Mother," she said, silently marveling at her composure. Her mother had not lifted her gaze from her needlework. With any luck, she could escape to her bedchamber. "The gathering was just family and close friends, but I managed to catch up with Regan. I still cannot believe she is a marchioness and a mother."

"And what of your escort, Lord Chillingsworth?" her mother said. She glanced up, but Emily turned away to suddenly admire the pair of Sèvres biscuit porcelain figures of Psyche and Cupid.

"What of him?" she said flippantly. She picked up Cupid. He was seated on a rock with his right finger touching his lips. His mischievous expression reminded her of Frost. She set down the forty-five-year-old figurine. "He fulfilled his duty as escort and then wandered off to join his friends."

"And that is all?"

Something in her mother's voice made her glance over her shoulder. Had she seen her and Frost arguing through one of the windows? "Why do you ask?"

Her mother's frown became more pronounced when she noticed her daughter's flushed face. "Emily, are you all right? You look as if you were—"

Emily waved aside her concern. "On the drive home, something . . . an eyelash or grit got into my eye. It hurt dreadfully, but my tears washed away the debris."

She was becoming rather adept at lying to her family.

The older woman patted the sofa cushion. "Sit beside me. The coloring in your face is quite off." She set her embroidery down, adjusted the spectacles perched on her nose, and studied her daughter's face.

Emily smiled and tried to laugh away her high coloring. "Too much sun, I confess. I should have chosen a different hat." She placed the hat on the table and sat down.

Her mother placed her hand on Emily's forehead. "You don't feel feverish. That is a good sign. You must show more care when wandering about in the sun. You are already twenty years old, you must look after your skin. I recommend that you have Mercy prepare a wash for your face. Crème de l'Enclos, I think." She began to tap her fingers as she recalled the ingredients. "Milk, white brandy, the juice of the lemon."

Whether she knew it or not, her mother's nagging was somehow soothing, even if it was annoying. "Mercy knows the recipe, Mother."

She wasn't listening. "Add the ingredients together and boil . . . then let the mixture cool before you use it. Use it night and day for a week."

Emily stood, preparing for escape. "Yes, Mother. I will give Mercy your instructions. Thank you."

Her younger sister, Judith, swaggered into the room. Perhaps it was a mean-spirited thought, but a year or two under Miss Swann's watchful eye would improve her sister's posture and gait.

"Gods, Em," Judith exclaimed as she noticed her sibling. "Your face is a fright!"

Emily retrieved her hat from the table. "Yes, thank you for your observation, Judith," she said drily, leaning down to kiss her mother's cheek. "Do not expect me for supper. I will ask Mercy to bring me a tray."

"Are you ill?" Her sister turned and followed Emily to the doorway. "You barely touched your plate this morning."

"I'm fine," she lied, unhappy that Judith was bringing up that small detail to their mother. Emily looked askance at the woman. "Was there anything before I retire?"

"So you are not joining us this evening?" her mother asked, not hiding her disappointment. "I managed to talk your father into coming along since we will be able to visit with my brother's family."

"Offer my uncle my apologies. Too much sun," Emily reminded her. "And I will not forget to use the wash."

"You don't want to end up with a leather face like Mrs. Rummage," her sister teased, poking at Emily's cheek.

"Quit it." She slapped Judith's hand away from her face.

The older woman sighed. "Yes . . . yes, that is important. Take care, my dear."

Emily turned to leave.

"Wait!" Her mother grimaced as she reached for her embroidery. "There was something I forgot to mention. You had several gentlemen callers this afternoon."

Her hat slipped from her fingers. "I did? There was?" She knelt down to collect her hat from the floor. "Who?"

The butler had left the silver tray on the table. Her mother picked up the calling cards and peered through her spectacles at the names. "Earl of Ashenhurst, Lord Macestone, and Mr. Halward. I daresay you have captured the *ton*'s attention, my dear. Your success reminds me of your sister. There were afternoons when the butler presented us with a small mountain of cards. Oh my, Lucy was so popular, this drawing room was often filled with eager suitors."

Emily ignored her mother's recollections of her sister's popularity as she considered the names her mother had mentioned. She recognized all three. Ashenhurst and Macestone were two of the young gentlemen Lord Chillingsworth had frightened off.

Before I knew he was Lucy's Frost.

She shook off the melancholy thought. "You mentioned Mr. Halward," she said.

Emily thought of their encounter at the park, and Frost's warning that the man was dangerous. "Did he say anything? Leave a message?"

Her mother paused, mildly peeved at the interruption. "He mentioned seeing you at the park this afternoon. Which I thought was rather odd since you were supposed to be at Lord and Lady Pashley's residence."

Ah, so that was the reason why she had been summoned. Her mother had thought she had caught her in a lie. Emily rolled her eyes in exasperation. "I was there. However, Lord Chillingsworth suggested a drive through the park since it was a lovely day. We encountered Mr. Halward, and he paid his respects. I cannot fathom why he called here."

She had not expected a reply from her mother, but she offered one anyway. "He said that he was looking forward to seeing you again."

Was it a warning? Emily doubted the man would have been brazen enough to have her mother deliver his threat. After Frost's warning, she was seeing villains everywhere.

Her mother retrieved her needle. "If you want my advice, I would leave Mr. Halward at the bottom of your pile of suitors."

"Why do you say that?"

"While I grant you he is wealthy, he is a commoner."

"Father is a commoner," Judith protested.

"Well, yes, but I think our Emily can aim higher. Take Lord Ashenhurst. He is young and titled, and I was impressed with his manners."

Her mother was impressed with his family connections and wealth. "Lord Ashenhurst is younger than I am."

Frost had called him a puppy.

"Only by a few years," her mother said, unwilling to view his youth as an obstacle. "You would do well to court his favor. Lord Macestone's, too."

Emily made a soft noncommittal sound in her throat.

"And let's not forget the delightful Lord Chillingsworth," her mother said cheerfully. To Judith, she added, "Such a charming gentleman. We should apply his name to the top of our list of suitors for Emily."

Appalled, she said, "Mother, Lord Chillingsworth is not courting me. The gentleman barely spoke to me at Regan's gathering."

Frost *had* kept his distance at his sister's house.

The older woman was not dissuaded by the news. "It was obvious to me that he liked you. A mother knows these things."

Emily gave up trying to convince her mother that she should strike Lord Chillingsworth from her list. She stomped off and went to search for her maid.

If her day didn't improve, she could always drown herself in a large bowl of face wash.

Chapter Fifteen

"It is rude to drink alone."

A dark green glass bottle of wine was placed before him on the table, and Frost looked up to see Lord Ravens standing in front of him. "Another six bottles and I will not care," he said indifferently, finishing his pot.

Frost beckoned the earl to join him. "Since when do you patronize the Golden Stag?"

"Oh, I have visited this place a time or two."

Lord Ravens deftly stepped aside so two burly men who were doing their best to murder each other could brawl without hindrance. A small group of spectators followed in the wake of their violence.

He sat down next to Frost so his back was to the wall. "Of course, I was younger and thought I was impervious to death."

"Ah, I recall those days as if they were yesterday," murmured Frost.

In truth, those wilder days did not seem too far in the distant past. In their youth, he and his friends had enjoyed countless evenings at the dark hell that was patronized by young noblemen with too much money, cheaters, weathered sailors, and criminals. They had placed wagers, drunk themselves blind, gambled, fought, and fucked whores in the private rooms in the back. Once the Lords of Vice had established Nox, their visits to the Golden Stag had waned. Only he and Saint, thirsting for reckless abandonment, had continued to visit on occasion, but that had ended with the marquess's marriage.

Frost still patronized the dangerous gambling hell, but most nights he arrived alone.

"This place is no better than a sty," Ravens observed, his fastidiousness and breeding on public display. "How can you stand the stench? More important, why are you not at Nox?"

He uncorked the bottle of wine and filled one of the empty pots. "I wanted to be alone."

"In a gambling hell?"

It sounded ridiculous even to Frost's ears. He poured some wine for himself. "At Nox, Berus would have watched over me like a benevolent father." The faithful steward would have led him upstairs and tucked him into bed so he could sleep off the brandy. The older man would have also tattled to his friends, whom he sensed were already concerned about him. "I was seeking another sort of companionship."

"Then it is a good thing that I found you before it was too late." Ravens sniffed at the wine before he took a tentative sip. He shuddered. "Vile. This stuff will eat away at your gut. Come. I have guests waiting for me at my house, and you shall be the guest of honor. Anything you desire shall be yours."

Frost immediately thought of Emily.

He could still see her tearstained face as she accused him of ruining her sister. Damn Lucy and her dying confession. *Even in death she was a selfish bitch,* he thought uncharitably.

"G'evening, Lord Chillingsworth." A plump blonde sauntered by the table.

Lord Ravens actually paled.

"Come," Ravens said sternly, taking Frost by the arm and hauling him to his feet. The wine bottle wobbled as the earl shoved the table to make room for their escape. "Someone has to rescue you before you do something foolish."

"Already have." Frost did not protest as he allowed the earl to drag him away. "I let her get under my skin."

"Then I will loan you my knife. It is small, sharp, and apt at removing the most troublesome splinters."

Ravens did not bother to inquire who the lady was. Perhaps he had already deduced which lady had driven his friend to risk his life at this particular den of iniquity.

Frost was touched by the earl's concern. He was not even remotely close to being drunk. Over the years, he had discovered that he had an impressive tolerance to anything fermented. However, when Colin Halward stepped in front of him, he staggered as he shook off Ravens's grip.

This was the man he had been waiting for.

"Halward. Most unexpected," Frost lied as he squinted at the man. "I thought the Golden Stag was too refined for someone like yourself?"

"Now, Frost, play nice. We were just leaving," the earl murmured.

Was he making excuses to Halward or reminding Frost that he could walk away? Either way, he did not care.

"I was most distressed to see Miss Cavell in your company this afternoon," Halward said to Frost, deciding to ignore Lord Ravens. "I made a point of sharing my concerns with her mother when I called at the house to pay my respects to the family."

Had Emily finally revealed her suspicions to her mother once she had run from him? It was obvious Emily had kept her sister's secrets from her family for the last five years. Otherwise, her mother would have ordered him from the house.

"Stay away from Miss Cavell and her family." Frost was several inches taller than Halward, and he moved forward to emphasize his threat. "The family has no sway in your grand schemes, so you can afford to be generous."

"I disagree. Miss Cavell's father is a respected barrister, and the mother is the daughter of Viscount Ketchen. Marrying their daughter would elevate my standing and open new doors for me."

The bastard had the audacity to grin at him.

"Cavell will never offer his daughter to a man who has ties to the criminal underworld, Halward. The cloying stench of the stews clings to your finely tailored coat. No amount of scent will cover it."

Now that he had warned him off from pursuing Emily, Frost was done with the man.

"Money forgives many sins, Chillingsworth,"

Halward drawled. "You above all people should know that I speak the truth."

Frost responded by slamming his fist into the man's mouth. Pain shot up his arm, but it was worth it. Halward staggered backward and landed on his arse. His eyes glinted with murderous intent as Frost and Ravens watched the man's mouth bleed and his lower lip swell.

"That might be rather difficult for a few days," Frost said, taking a clean handkerchief from his coat pocket and tossing it at Halward. "You might want to tend to that cut on your lip."

The man ignored the handkerchief. "You might do well to watch your back."

"Why should I when you seem capable of the task?" Frost countered, deliberately offering Halward his back. He was not worried about the man seeking revenge in front of a room filled with witnesses.

As he walked away from the injured man, he murmured to his companion, "Well, that was gratifying."

Ravens shot him a startled look. "Then your expectations are miserably low. Let's see if I can improve upon them."

Lord Ravens's elixir for a gent sulking over a female was to prove that the world was full of surrogates. Most days, Frost would have heartily approved of the cure. Over the years, how many times had he lectured his friends that no chit was worth a sour stomach and headache?

As much as he loathed to admit it, his relationship

with Miss Cavell was different. The charges she had leveled at him were grave and cast him into a despicable light. For the first time in his life, he could claim innocence—but Emily did not believe him. Neither would he, if he had been in her position. The reputation he had nurtured and relished was being used against him.

He was well and truly enraged about it.

Punching Halward helped. Frost despised the man for setting his sights on Nox, but his depraved interest in Emily had provoked Frost to violence. He should have thanked the man for being so obliging.

"Ah, I see your mood has improved," Ravens said, slumping into one of the nearby chairs with the grace of a panther. "I trust you are enjoying the brandy."

"Always," Frost assured him. The richly appointed interior of the earl's library reminded him of his position. Of the influence he wielded. Halward was a worm to be crushed beneath his heel, even if he alone had to see to the task. "I am also savoring the bruises on my knuckles. I gained a certain satisfaction in cracking Halward's teeth."

"About that," Ravens said, his visage growing serious. "I have heard vague rumors about the man. If any of them are true, it is best to avoid tangling with him. He has more to prove than his manhood, my friend."

"He is mingling with decent people, Ravens," Frost argued. Like Emily and her family. "People who can be hurt by the man's ambition and greed."

"Are you a decent fellow?" the earl mocked.

"Most people would disagree." Frost shrugged.

"However, I cannot abide people of Halward's ilk. Sadly, it appears, with maturity even I have developed certain standards of conduct."

"A pity," his friend lamented. "I, however, never intend to grow up."

Frost laughed. "Aye, I must confess, I cannot imagine the sour-faced matrons of the *ton* introducing you to their daughters."

"And they open their doors to you? Hypocrite," Ravens said, taking a sip of his wine. "Your very nature is steeped in depravity and sin. You would not know how to exist without it."

Frost thought of his parents. While Regan could barely recall their father, nonetheless he was old enough to remember him. Much like Hunter and Grace, his parents' marriage had been arranged by their parents. While there was affection between the couple, once Frost had been born, neither one had let fidelity stand in their way. There had been an endless parade of lovers and mistresses for both of them.

Although it was accepted without question that his father had perished in a hunting accident, Frost had often wondered if it was his sire's reckless nature that had claimed his life. And while it was likely that his mother would continue to plague him, he considered it a small blessing that Regan had not inherited the family's more unpleasant traits. She was pure of heart and he intended her to stay that way.

Frost raised his glass to Lord Ravens. "You are probably right," he said, silently toasting the man he was, flaws and all.

Ravens brightened at the sound of the door opening. He leaned his head back and greeted the three ladies who had entered. "Ah, there you are. Ladies, we have been drinking away our sorrows and despairing for the lack of good company. Pray save us!"

"Lord Ravens, you have been a reclusive host this evening," the redhead said, boldly kissing him on the mouth. "We feared you had found other amusements."

"Not when I had learned of your arrival," the earl said, nonchalantly clasping her hand. "Faith, have you been introduced to my good friend Frost?"

Ravens never troubled himself with titles or surnames. Most of the people who arrived at his door preferred discretion.

The gray-eyed redhead scrutinized him from head to toe. She apparently liked what she saw. "A pleasure, Frost."

She held out her hand, and he accepted it without getting up. "Good evening, Faith," he said, assessing the woman before him.

Faith, if that was truly her real name, was older than the redhead who had occupied his thoughts all day. He guessed the woman's age to be closer to his. She was pretty, but her mouth was a little too generous for her face. He was grateful there was nothing about her that reminded him of Emily.

"The enchanting blonde on my lap is Charity," Ravens said, rubbing her backside. "Thankfully, the lady is as generous as her name."

Faith slid down next to him, and her dark-haired friend flanked his other side. A ghost of a smile curved

Frost's lips as the ladies shifted closer. "I hope you were not burdened with the name Chastity, my dear," he said to the brunette.

"I'm Blythe," she said, smiling up into his face.

"I can see that you are," Frost murmured. "Ravens, you have outdone yourself."

"I usually do," he boasted. The blonde had managed to untie Ravens's cravat and undo the top buttons of his shirt.

Frost appreciated the small distraction his friend had arranged. Ravens had even procured a redhead to replace the one who now despised him, another reminder that females could be exchanged as easily as waistcoats.

The two females beside him moved in unison. Faith laid her hand on his face and guided his mouth to hers, while Blythe curled up next to him and placed her hand on his crotch.

His body hardened in reaction.

It was a natural response. One he wasn't ashamed of. Women were inspiring, after all, and the two on each side of him were making their intentions clear.

Frost politely ended the kiss by turning his head aside, thinking it was unfair for him to have two wenches when his host only possessed the one. Ravens, however, was not paying attention to him, since he and the blonde had gotten straight to business. Charity had straddled the earl and was riding him at a leisurely pace. For his part, Ravens had unfastened the woman's dress and bared her generous breasts.

He started as a nimble female hand had closed

around his semi-erect cock. Faith reached for his cravat, pausing only to lean across him to give Blythe an open-mouth kiss.

For the man in the middle, he felt disconnected from everything. This was not the first occasion that he and Ravens had spent the evening fucking females. He was comfortable with his body. Ravens and various Lords of Vice had glimpsed his muscled arse over the years as they had shared women.

He could not even quibble about the two wenches determined to bed him. They were pretty and certainly knew what they wanted. He enjoyed all types of women, and the nights he could bed more than one, he felt blessed.

So why was he hesitating? His cock was still soft in the woman's skillful hands. Any other night, he would have bent the brunette over the nearest chair and pounded into her until both of them screamed with pleasure. Then he would have grabbed the redhead and showed her the meaning of endurance. So why was he not fucking himself into a state of exhaustion where Emily's tearstained face could not haunt him?

The answer hit him like a punch.

He did not want just any woman. Frost wanted Emily. No substitute would satisfy him. "No," he said gently, removing the brunette's hand from inside his trousers. He stilled Faith's hands.

Frost had never found himself in this particular predicament. He had been attracted to other women in the past, but the feeling never lasted. Even when he felt the first stirrings of lust, he could always turn to an available woman to satisfy them.

"My apologies, ladies."

Faith and Blythe groaned in disappointment as he stood up. He took a moment to adjust himself before he refastened the side buttons on his trousers. He wanted Emily, but felt trapped by the restrictions imposed on him by the *ton,* Regan, his own damn honor. Even Emily was insisting that he should not follow his true nature.

To hell with all of them.

To make amends, Frost clasped each lady's hand in turn and kissed it. "I will leave you in Ravens's hands. Don't fret, I am positive he will be up to the task."

Ravens was too distracted for explanations, so Frost didn't bother.

He slipped away into the night. There was only one lady he craved, and he was tired of fighting his nature.

Chapter Sixteen

Emily awoke with a start. She thought she heard a noise, but she must have been dreaming. Or so it seemed, until a large hand covered her mouth.

"Don't scream," Frost whispered in her ear.

Emily bit him. It was only fair, since he had frightened her half to death. Her fists shot out and she punched him. Most of them were glancing blows, but one caught him on the chin.

He grunted in pain.

"Christ!" He pulled her against him. "Stop that. Promise me you won't scream, and I will release you."

She nodded.

"On your honor?"

Again she nodded, this time speaking against his hand. Frost could not understand her, but her tone must have assured him. Slowly he removed his hand, as if he did not quite trust her.

It stung. She was the one who should be questioning *his* honor.

"There is no point in screaming. My family is out for the evening and the servants are upstairs. I doubt they would hear me," she grumbled, then tensed as she decided that it was foolhardy to admit that she was on her own.

"May I light a candle?" he asked politely.

Emily stared at him in the darkness and sighed. She had been miserable all evening. Her parting with Frost had been painful, and while she thought she had gained the answers to her unspoken questions, new ones had taken the place of the old.

"Let me do it," she grumbled, climbing out of her bed. "You will break something I treasure."

Like my heart.

It took her a few minutes to find what she needed to light the candle. Unused to the bright flame, she blinked as her eyes adjusted to the light. She picked up the brass candleholder and moved to join him.

"How did you get into my bedchamber?" Another question gave her pause. "How did you know which room was mine?"

Good heavens, what if he had found his way into Judith's bedchamber? Her sister had a strong pair of lungs. If she had been in bed, her screams would have awakened the entire street.

"Your family is careless about locking up the house," he explained, scowling at her. "This isn't the country, Emily. There are dangers in this town."

"So you keep telling me," she said before she glanced down and remembered that she was wearing her nightgown. Emily gasped. "You can't be here and see me like this. I don't care how you found me. You have to go!"

"I can't," he said, his gaze following her every

movement. "Besides, I approve of what you are wearing."

Emily growled at him. She actually growled in frustration at his stubbornness. Placing the candleholder on the table beside her bed, she stomped over to the other side of the room. Her maid had placed an extra blanket on the chair. Emily seized it and wrapped it around her body.

"You, sir, are no gentleman," she said, glaring at him. How could she be so happy to see him when he was so maddening?

"No, you called me a scoundrel and you are correct. I have little respect for rules unless they are my own. I don't play fair." His turquoise-blue gaze glowed in the candlelight. "And you are completely at a disadvantage when you tangle with me."

He was blatantly honest for a scoundrel. "So how does a lady best you?"

"You don't," he said with his usual bluntness. "However, there might be way for both of us to win."

"How so?"

He offered her one of his angelic smiles. "Despite your initial anger, you are pleased to see me."

"No."

"Yes," he countered. "Do you know how I can tell?"

The question seemed innocent enough, but she sensed a trap. "No," she said, nibbling on the bait anyway.

Frost patted the mattress, inviting her to sit beside him. She moved closer, wondering how long he had been in her room. Had he watched over her as she slept? He had managed to slip into her bed, and she had been blissfully unaware until he had decided to wake her.

How often did he slip into bedchambers?

Emily wasn't certain she wanted to know the answer to that particular question. She sat down on the mattress.

"That's more comfortable." He took her hand. It was then that she noticed that his hands were as bare as hers. "If I were a gentleman, I would tell you that I saw your delight in your expressive face and eyes. However, you are aware of my true nature so I feel free to reveal the truth." He paused, as if he was trying not to laugh. "It was your body."

"My—" She glanced down at the blanket wrapped around her. "What?"

Laughter bubbled forth like a natural spring. "Forgive me. It was rude of me to look, but you aren't wearing stays. In fact, you aren't wearing much at all."

Emily huffed and offered him her back as she opened the blanket that covered her breasts. Even she could not ignore how her nipples poked at the fabric of her nightgown or the dark shadow of the hair between her legs.

"You are despicable."

"If you say so," he happily agreed. "I think you are beautiful."

Emily repositioned the blanket before she shifted around to face him again. Good grief, how could any man be so handsome? How could any lady resist him when he was being so charming?

She stilled.

Was she following the same path as Lucy?

"Stop it," he ordered.

Emily scowled at him. "I beg your pardon?"

Frost scooted closer to her so he could cup her face with his hands. "Stop thinking. Your assumptions always get you in trouble."

"How do you know?

He rolled his eyes. "You are as guileless as a babe, Emily. I can see the questions and doubt and, yes, even fear in your hazel eyes." His thumb caressed her chin. "I wasn't thinking about the right or wrong of it when I came here this evening. I just needed to see you. I couldn't allow Lucy's last coherent word stand between us, especially when it is a lie."

Emily had observed the incensed disbelief on his face when she had told him. His reaction had not been feigned. It was her feelings for him and her sister that had muddled her brain. "Frost—"

He silenced her with his thumb. "Hush. Just listen. I was telling you the truth. Aye, I knew Lucy. I had encountered her on several occasions. She was beautiful, seemed to gather a small flock of admirers wherever she went, which suited her because she was a consummate flirt."

Taking exception to the last part, Emily's lips parted to chastise him. "I—"

"I'm not finished," he said brusquely, but his fingers caressed her cheek in apology for the anger she heard in his voice. "Lucy was never my lover. You have to believe me."

God help her, she wanted to believe him. "Frost, your name was the last word she spoke before she died."

Frustration darkened his face. "Is it possible that you misheard her?"

Emily shook her head.

Frost brought his hand to his face and pressed his fingers to his eyebrows as if his head was paining him. His hand fell away and his eyes snapped open, locking on to hers. "I have no explanation as to why your sister said my name. I need you to believe me when I swear to you that I was not the man who seduced and abandoned her."

"I do," she said, gasping when he pulled her to him and roughly embraced her. "I still don't understand why you didn't—?"

"Bed your sister? While it pains me to tarnish my rather notorious reputation as a first-rate scoundrel—I couldn't."

Belatedly, Emily noticed that Frost was dressed in his evening clothes. Had he attended a ball? Had he been searching for her? Or perhaps black seemed appropriate since he had recently taken up the occupation of housebreaker.

"It is inappropriate to ask, but I must know—why couldn't you? Lucy was so beautiful." Emily could have flogged herself for reminding him of her sister's beauty.

A small, selfish part of her was so jealous that Lucy had the pleasure of meeting Frost first that she did not know whether she could bear it if he agreed with her.

Tenderness softened the harsh lines in his face. "Isn't it obvious, Miss Emily Cavell . . . I was waiting for you."

Frost slowly lowered his head until their lips were an inch apart. "May I kiss you?"

He was asking for permission? She suspected that when it came to women, he always took what he wanted. Their previous kisses confirmed it. His gaze ensnared her, silently begging her to grant him the liberties he craved.

It was difficult to nod with his hands caging her face. "Yes. I would like that very much."

Emily started at the electrical spark that stung her upper lip when he brushed his lips against hers.

"The blanket," she laughed, thinking of the friction game she had played with her siblings when she was younger. Wool blankets were rather effective for generating the painful spark.

His beautiful hands drifted down to her shoulders. "Let's get rid of it," Frost said, slipping it from her shoulders. Nor did he give her a chance to remember that her nightgown did a poor job concealing her body. His mouth was as powerful as the jars of mysterious potent powders the chemist on Bond Street stored on his shelves.

Emily felt drugged as his lips rubbed and nibbled. It seemed natural to part her lips and allow his tongue to slide against her own. It was a lazy sensual dance of flesh as he murmured his approval when she mimicked his actions.

She felt the mattress hit her back. She had not even realized she was falling. Frost followed her, pressing her into the comforting softness of her bed. As she arched up to capture his lips again, the hand curving around her hip gradually slid up her waist, and then upward to the underside of her breast.

"Damn!"

Emily opened her eyes, but he was already gone. She rolled onto her stomach to see him head for the door. The sound of the lock clicking into place guaranteed their privacy. Through slumberous eyes she watched him remove his black evening coat. Next, his waistcoat. Both garments ended up on the seat of the chair.

Frost returned to the bed. He offered her an apologetic smile. "Sorry. Now, where was I?"

Emily rolled onto her back and laughed. "I believe you were here." She was planning to touch her lips but changed her mind. Impulsively, she reached for his hand and brought it to her waist. It seemed too brazen to place it on her breast.

"Ah, yes," he said, the anticipation in his voice making her blush. "Though I was thinking about placing my hand . . . here."

"Oh." She squirmed as his fingers measured the shape and fullness of her left breast.

"And this." He lowered his head, and she felt the warmth of his breath over her nipple.

The sensitive flesh pebbled in response. Emily moaned as he dampened the thin fabric of her nightgown with an open kiss over her nipple. She felt the flat rasp of the side of his tongue and shuddered.

"Breathe, Emily," he teased. He unfastened the

glass buttons at her throat. “I don’t want you to faint on me.”

He flashed a wicked grin at her as he shifted to pay attention to her other breast. “At least, not yet.”

Could a lady faint from pleasure?

Emily is a virgin, gent.

Frost knew he should keep his hands off her, but he couldn’t resist tasting her. The thin linen of her nightgown moistened against his tongue. As a rule, it was wise to stay away from innocents. The chits were too young to understand the difference between lust and love, and the consequences of surrendering to their passions.

The tragic tale usually ended with angry fathers and threats of marriage. Aye, for a man who did not have marriage on his mind, it was better to pursue ladies who understood the difference.

Like the wenches Ravens had pushed at him.

Frost had felt their eager hands on him and seen the lust in their eyes, and he wanted nothing to do with them. He wanted Emily. He would gladly trade a taste of the woman he desired for a night of wicked shagging with twenty women.

The insight thumped him like a rock on the head.

He lifted his face from her breast and stared into Emily’s hazel gaze. Green and gold melded into brown, and her shy wonderment made him dizzy. He could kill for this woman, he thought. Smite any man for touching her.

Christ, he should have one of his friends beat him

for dallying with her. "You should tell me to leave," he said, his voice thick with emotion.

"Here." Emily tugged at the ends of his cravat. "Your valet must have been tied this with his eyes closed."

One of the women at Ravens's house had ruined the pressed folds and knot, and in his haste to leave he had clumsily retied it. He had not even bothered with the buttons on his shirt.

The thought of Emily touching the other woman's handiwork seemed abhorrent. He sat up on his knees. "Allow me," he said, tearing at the knot and half choking himself. He offered her a lopsided grin as he gathered up the length of fabric and threw it over the side of the bed. With his fingers, he reached for the edge of his collar and pulled, popping the remaining buttons from their moorings.

Emily giggled as the glass buttons struck the floor. "Your tailor must adore you."

"Everyone adores me, my dear lady," he teased, bending down to kiss her on the mouth. "Now stop distracting me. Seducing you takes all of my wits, and you have a bad habit of scattering them."

"How am I to blame?" she sputtered, laughing hysterically when he caressed her stomach with his fingers. "Stop . . . that tickles!"

Frost braced his left arm above her head. "Well, that won't do," he said, deliberately tickling her again. "I was seeking a different response from you."

To test her resolve and his, he flattened his hand on her lower belly. The muscles rippled beneath her flesh as she tried not to laugh. A mischievous smile tugged at his lips as he slid his hand lower to the shadowed apex of her thighs.

Emily sucked in her breath as he stroked her. He kept his touch light, reverent. He did not wish to frighten her.

"Does this feel good?"

She nodded wordlessly. Her body was a temple that was fashioned to be worshiped. Frost kissed her belly. His tongue traced the diameter of the indentation of her navel. Her muscles contracted, but this time she didn't giggle. Distracted by his sensual ministrations, she had not noticed that he had pushed the hem of her nightgown higher, exposing most of her thigh. His fingers quested farther until he reached the copper curls that concealed the soft feminine folds between her legs.

Emily held her breath at his tentative caress.

"Breathe," he reminded her again. His own breath caught in his chest when he took in the heady musk of her arousal. Tucked away in his trousers, his cock lengthened and hardened until it was impossible to conceal the evidence of his lust.

Despite her innocence, Emily desired him. Her body responded so sweetly to his touch that he wanted to howl like an animal heavy with need for his mate. He wanted to roll her over and cover her with his body while his fingers parted her folds and readied her for his cock.

"Frost," she gasped, nearly sitting up when he penetrated her with his finger. She tried to cover herself when he eased her back onto the bed.

"Let me touch you," he murmured, calming her

with kisses. "There is no reason to fear the pleasure I can give you."

To prove it, he stroked her and she trembled. Modesty caused her to press her thighs together, thus trapping his hand. "I will not take anything that you are not willing to give. There are ways I can pleasure you that will not take your innocence."

The pressure of her thighs eased, but she had yet to open to him fully. "I don't know about this, Frost," she said, her eyes dark with fear and arousal. "My sister—"

She was worried that she might end up a ruined lady like her sister. Not that he could blame her. It had ended badly for Lucy. And while he had not slipped into her bedchamber to steal her virginity, he was honest enough to admit that he was sorely tempted to toss aside his good intentions and honor.

His body ached for completion. He longed to strip off the rest of his clothes, part her hips with his body, and push his cock into her wet sheath. He wanted to be the man to rid Emily of her maidenhead so he could fill her, savoring her first taste of passion, and show her that he could take her to those lofty heights again. Over and over, until his cries of completion mingled with hers.

"Only pleasure, Emily," he said, amused that he sounded so damn honorable. In truth, touching her would bring him pleasure, as well. He wiggled his fingers to remind her that his hand was still buried in her nest of curls. "I will halt on your orders. I promise." He gave her a pained smile. "But only if you mean it."

"Already adding conditions to your promise, I see," she said with a tremulous smile.

"Well, I am only looking after your best interests, my dear," Frost lightly teased.

Emily managed to startle him by reaching out suddenly and touching his cheek. "I trust you, Frost."

She leaned forward and kissed him. It was sweetly chaste, and he felt it all the way down to his knees.

Until that moment, it had never occurred to Frost that the lady in his arms had the power to break his heart.

Chapter Seventeen

Hours ago, she had gone to bed, heartsick and empty, trying not to believe that Frost was her sister's seducer. How much had changed since she had awakened to find the infuriating man in her bedchamber. Not only was he demanding that she believe him when he vowed he had nothing to do with Lucy's ruination, he was asking her to trust him with her body as well.

If he intended to take my virginity, he would have done so.

Although she had limited knowledge of the ways of lovemaking, Emily could sense Frost was holding a part of himself back. He kissed her on the mouth and the breasts, touched her intimately between her legs, and promised her nothing but pleasure. Instead of removing his trousers and shirt, he had remained dressed while she was laid out in her revealing nightgown like a wanton goddess.

"Does touching me hurt you?" she asked, stealing a glance at the blatant display of his manhood. She had never seen him in such a state, and wondered if he was in pain.

"Only if you deny me," he quipped. "I desire you, Emily. Let me love you."

It was an odd choice of words for a man who considered himself a Lord of Vice. "Would you like me to remove my nightgown?" she asked, staring at him shyly through a veil of red hair.

"So you intend to add to my torment, eh?"

"What? No," she insisted, sitting up. Emily stared down at the front of her nightgown. The linen was still damp from his mouth, forming rings around her nipples. "You have asked to touch me. I merely assumed my nightgown was barring your way."

"The glimpses of your delectable flesh tempt and seduce me," he said, placing his hands over hers. "I long to touch you without any hindrance, but it is your choice."

Her choice.

Frost had come to her, knowing he was asking the impossible. He sought her trust and her body, but he was leaving the decision in her hands. It would have been simpler if he had just taken control. By consenting, she was taking on some of the blame.

It was a cunning stratagem.

Coming to a decision, she lifted the hem of the nightgown, revealing her body to him as she pulled the garment over her head. Though she could feel the heat of his gaze, Frost made no attempt to help her.

He was silent as she placed the wadded nightgown on the mattress. After a minute, she began to squirm under his scrutiny. "Well," she said, raising her hand to cover her breasts.

Frost caught her hands. Her eyes widened as she felt him tremble. "You are exquisite. Perfection." He kissed her hands. "And I desire you so much I fear I might embarrass myself."

"How so?"

"Never mind." He kissed her nose. "It is a torment I happily embrace if it means that I can put my hands on you."

To prove it, Frost stretched her out onto the bed. He settled down beside her. He ignored the bulge protruding at the front of his trousers. Instead he leaned over and kissed her eyelids. His touch was as light as butterfly wings, and it made her smile.

"Do I get to touch you?" she asked with her eyes closed, even though he had moved down to her cheekbones.

"No."

Her eyes flew open at the harshness in his voice.

"Don't ask this of me," he said curtly. "My need is too great. Just lie back and enjoy the pleasure I can give you."

"It does not seem very fair," she muttered.

"You should enjoy watching me suffer," he replied, nibbling on her neck. "Denial is good for my soul."

Even so, he did not seem to be suffering the pangs as he freely explored her body. With his mouth and hands, he left no inch of her flesh untouched.

She hissed in surprise when he delicately bit the

visible line of her collarbone, but Frost was far from finished. As she arched her back, his mouth moved to her breast. She gasped and longed to push him away as he suckled at her. Instead, she threaded her fingers through his dark hair. Touching him calmed her. He licked her nipple, and she slowly became aware of the dampness between her legs. Her breasts tingled and the sensation was nothing she had ever experienced.

"You must stop."

Frost paused and met her worried gaze. "Why, dear lady?"

"Something is wrong."

Frost grinned at her. "Show me where you ache. Is it here?" He cupped her other breast and lightly squeezed.

"Yes."

His hand moved to her belly. "What about here?"

Emily nodded. "A bit, and lower," she admitted, concern warring with shame.

"Ah," he said, the intensity in his blue gaze spellbinding. "Guide my hand and show me."

Awkwardly, she covered the hand he had resting on her stomach and directed him to the wetness clinging to the hair between her legs. "This is—"

Not normal, she thought.

"Desire, Emily." Beneath her hand, his fingers sought the sensitive flesh protected within her feminine folds. "It is primal, disturbing, chaotic, and most of all, it is pleasure. The sort that shoots you straight into the heavens, shatters you into a million pieces, and then puts you together again. Once you have experienced it, you will never be the same person."

She gasped.

"Your body is aroused and hungers for completion. What you are feeling is healthy and natural. You needn't fear it," he whispered seductively. "Stop fighting it. Now close your eyes."

Emily knew it was futile to argue with him, so she complied. Perhaps if she could not see him, she could manage the overwhelming feelings his kisses and caresses evoked. She shivered, not understanding how she could be cold when her flesh burned under the scorching heat of his breath.

"That's right, love," he said, approvingly. "Move your leg. Aye, like that. Just concentrate on the pleasure."

She smiled as he lightly bit her hipbone. His manhood pressed against her thigh as he positioned himself between her legs. He had promised her that he sought only to please her, but the hard length of masculine flesh reminded her that Frost was denying himself his own release.

"Touch yourself . . . here." He guided her hands to her breasts. "When you are alone, have you ever caressed yourself?"

"No!"

He chuckled. "You should. It is no sin to learn how you like to be touched. It would please me, knowing that you were thinking of me when you touched your breasts or rubbed the sweet little nubbin . . . ah, *here*."

Frost demonstrated with his mouth. Emily sucked in her breath and tried to twist away from the brazen claiming, but he was stronger. He simply grabbed her hips and held her in place.

How did he expect her to endure?

Every time she moved, he used each wiggle to deepen his incredibly blatant kisses on the most intimate parts of her body. She had never imagined a man would touch her like this and enjoy it. Frost moaned with undisguised pleasure as he licked and teased the tender flesh and folds.

Emily tried to remember to breathe. Her hands covered her aching breasts as she felt a flutter within her womb. Frost drank from the heart of her as if her desire flowed as freely as wine. What he was doing to her was shameful. She should tell him to stop. The words were stuck in her throat as he stroked her with his skillful fingers and that nimble tongue.

Then she suddenly could not think at all.

The warmth pooling in her loins ignited into flames. Emily cried out, her head whipping from side to side as Frost's relentless claiming consumed her. Her womb clenched almost painfully, and intuitively she knew this man could ease the exquisite agony. She raised her hips off the bed and wholly gave herself to him.

The tension that had racked Emily's entire body gradually waned. She was breathless and weak, even though she had done little but savor the pleasure Frost had wrung from her body.

"That was just a taste?" she asked in disbelief, her loins still quivering with residual energy from her release.

Frost wiped his mouth on his sleeve and crawled up to recline next to her. He looked quite pleased with himself. "Aye, it is just the beginning. And I've kept my word. I promised pleasure and you're still a virgin."

Emily had not given her virginity a thought when he had put his mouth on her. It was the danger of passion, she supposed. The pleasure given and received was so immense that when a person was ensnared, they would do anything to keep it.

Though, she thought as she frowned, she had not given him anything. Emily rolled onto her side and glanced at the proof of his desire. "Frost, what about you? You haven't—"

She tried to touch the thick bulge at the front of his trousers, but he swiftly moved away from her.

"Don't," he commanded as he sat up on the mattress. "My control is tenuous, Emily, and I am trying to be honorable."

"Honorable men do not sneak into a lady's bedchamber."

His lips twitched with humor. "I suppose you are right. However, you can trust me to keep my promises."

Emily sat up and grabbed her nightgown, using it to cover herself. "Does it hurt?" She could not keep the worry out of her voice.

Frost's harsh expression softened at her question. "Yes, but I will survive. You needn't fret about me." He reached for his waistcoat.

He was leaving.

She sat in the middle of her bed, feeling drained and uncertain. "You could stay awhile."

"I can't, Emily." He walked over to her, fastening the buttons on the waistcoat. "If one of the servants caught us, or your family . . ." He shrugged. "It was reckless of me to come to you like this, but I could not help myself. Even so, I would not see you hurt because of my selfishness."

She nibbled her lip. "Are you leaving because we—I mean you—"

He spared her from asking the uncomfortable question. "No. I want to stay with you. Christ, don't make it any harder than it is."

Emily covered her mouth with her hand as she burst into a fit of giggles. She couldn't help it.

Frost's eyes gleamed as his laughter blended with hers. "Witch," he said affectionately. He kissed the tip of her nose. "I can assure you, *it* couldn't get any harder."

He pressed a firm kiss on her mouth and moved away to collect his evening coat. "Put your nightgown on before I change my mind."

"Will I—?" It seemed foolish to ask when they might meet again.

"What?" Frost glanced up. He smoothed the fabric down on his left sleeve.

"My mother mentioned something about attending the theater this week. Will I . . . see you there, perhaps?" she asked, praying she didn't sound dreadfully pathetic.

"Of course." He paused and noted her expression. "What? Did you think you've seen the last of me? Not a chance."

Chapter Eighteen

Frost regretted the necessity of leaving her.

He congratulated himself on the control he had been able to exert when he had introduced Emily to her first taste of passion. The need to find his release in her sweet, warm body had almost been too much bear. His still-semi-erect cock was proof that her scent was calling to him. It clung to his fingers, coated his face and tongue, and lingered in his nostrils. If gaining her trust had not been so important, he would have proved that he could be a scoundrel and taken her virginity. To hell with his promises. As her body shimmered with the lingering effects of her release, he could have opened his trousers and pressed the head of his cock against the yielding opening of her sheath.

Emily would not have refused him. He had seen the need in her eyes. As he walked through the front door of his residence, he told himself that he was a good man . . . an honorable man.

Frost glanced up to see Regan standing in the front hall.

"Why, good evening, brat. What are you—"

Regan marched up to him and slapped him hard across the face.

"All of these years," his sister raged. "How could you?"

She raised her hand to strike him again, but he captured her wrist. "What is it? What's happened?" Frost asked, baffled that Regan was so determined to maim him.

The answer came to him almost immediately.

His mother had revealed herself to her daughter. He could happily murder the hateful bitch.

Frost hauled Regan into his arms and hugged her close. She fought him, impotently pounding at his chest. "Listen to me. I can explain." Then she went limp in his arms and sobbed uncontrollably.

He glanced up to see Dare standing in the doorway of the library. His brother-in-law's enigmatic expression revealed how much of a mess he had created for himself. Frost also noticed that the marquess had two glasses of brandy in his hands. If he was a true friend, one of those glasses was for him.

He would definitely need one after he had soothed his sister's feelings.

"Whoreson," she mumbled against the front of Frost's coat.

Frost thought the charge was fitting.

Fifteen minutes later, a calmer Regan sat in one of the chairs in his library. After her angry outburst, she had gone upstairs to wash her face. Frost was relieved to see upon her return that she was no longer crying. Regan was not the sort of lady who cried to manipulate those around her to get her way. When she cried, it was sincere, messy, and violent.

She broke his heart.

Dare had not pressed him for answers while they had waited for Regan. Frost was also grateful that his friend had not punched him for making his wife cry.

"You shouldn't have kept this from me," she lashed out at him.

"Obviously, I disagreed," he drily replied. "The lady abandoned us. I saw no reason to involve you."

"Involve me?" Regan looked as stunned as he had been when he had discovered that their mother still lived. She took a sip of the brandy her husband had pressed into her hand, even though she thought the stuff was vile. It proved how rattled she was by the news. "Frost, this is our mother. How long have you known the truth?"

Frost hesitated. His gaze shifted to Dare, and the man had the audacity to shrug. It was his friend's way of telling him that he was leaving the decision up to him.

There was no reason not to tell her the truth. "I learned of our mother's miraculous resurrection a year before I sent you away to Miss Swann's Academy."

He tensed when his sister's lip trembled, but she managed to hold on to her composure.

"When you sent me away, I thought you didn't want me underfoot, disrupting your life," she said wearily.

Her admission was a kick to his heart. Although he refused to admit it, he had regretted sending her away. At the time, he had thought he had been doing the right thing. Her infatuation with Dare had given him the perfect excuse to take action.

Frost scrubbed his face and thought of Emily, warm and asleep in her bed. At the moment, he would gladly toss his good intentions aside for another hour in her arms. However, that would have only put off the inevitable. Regan was feeling betrayed, and he had his mother to thank for this mess. "Utter nonsense. It killed me to send you away."

"Then why . . ." Her voice trailed off. "You sent me away so *she* couldn't find me."

"Our mother abandons us to run off with her married lover, and I'm the cold, soulless blackguard," he complained to Dare. "Let's forget the fact that I was young and had no idea how to look after a young girl properly."

"Frost, I know you did your best." Her face crumpled. "It was just a shock to see her sitting in my drawing room as if nothing had happened. After all of these years, she seemed so happy to see me. She wanted to meet Dare and Bishop. Then she began telling me that you have been keeping us apart for years. I was so confused when she finally left."

"Did she ask you for money?"

Startled, she gasped. "What are you talking about?"

"Money," he said succinctly. "It is all our mother has ever wanted. I have been sending payments to her man of affairs for years. The only reason she approached you was to punish me for not giving her more."

"You've been paying her to stay away."

"It seemed like a reasonable condition to our

original arrangement. You were so young when our father died, and then our mother disappeared. I was relieved when I heard that she had drowned. Her death gave you a chance to grieve and move on. Did she tell you that she approached me years ago, only to be turned away?"

Her silence confirmed his suspicions.

"She failed to mention that she came to me because she was lacking in funds. Her current lover had abandoned her, and she needed money to ensnare another poor fool."

"You make her sound like—"

"What? A whore?" he sneered. "I have more respect for a prostitute. Our mother accepted my terms and turned her back on you without shedding a single tear of regret. You might want to remember that the next time you allow her near your son."

Leaning against the edge of Frost's desk, Dare stirred from his stance. "I believe you, Frost."

"Thank you," he huffed. Frost had dealt with enough people who had challenged his intentions this evening.

Regan had a miserable look on her face. He wanted to throttle their mother for upsetting Regan. She had won the battle, but he was not finished with the woman.

"It's not that I don't believe what you are telling me is true."

Frost winced, trying not to be hurt by the lingering doubt he heard in her voice. "Feel free to visit my solicitor if you need proof," he said, sounding as if he didn't care one way or the other.

"Your word is good enough for us," Dare said. "Once Regan calms down, she'll realize that you were just trying to protect her."

His friend's words eased the tension in Frost's gut. "You sound certain."

"I am." Dare grinned. "If you recall, you even tried to protect her from me."

Frost snorted. "And don't think I don't often regret it, gent."

Regan shot up from her chair and dashed straight into his arms. He hesitated, and then wrapped his arms around her. "I don't doubt you. I just think your anger has colored your opinion of our mother. There is a possibility that she regrets the decisions she has made."

Doubtful.

"I won't stop you from seeing her." Frost ignored Dare's soft choke of laughter. No one controlled Regan. Especially not the men in her life. "I don't want to see you hurt."

She nodded, her cheek pressed against his chest. "I know. I love you, Frost."

He rubbed the top of her head with his chin. "I love you, too, brat."

Chapter Nineteen

The next afternoon, one of Frost's servants delivered a bouquet of chrysanthemums to the Cavell residence. The footman handed Lord Chillingsworth's card to the butler, and said the flowers were for Miss Cavell.

"How odd," her mother said when she had come to admire the flowers. "All the blooms are red."

"What is wrong with red?" Emily demanded. Frost had sent her flowers. She was pleased by his thoughtfulness.

"Nothing. It is a lovely color," her mother said, plucking one of the blooms from the vase and reinserting it until she was satisfied with the arrangement. "One expects some variety, that's all."

"Red hair."

Emily glanced over at her father, who was occupied with his paper. "Were you speaking to us, Father?"

Her sixty-year-old father peered over the top of his paper. "This man who sent you the flowers. It is to pay homage to your hair." He set down his paper. "By the by, who is this gentleman?"

Her sister sat at one of the tables near the windows writing a letter. "Lord Chillingsworth. He is Emily's suitor."

"He is not my suitor," Emily weakly protested. She could not imagine Frost courting anyone. "He is a friend. Do you recall me mentioning Lady Regan? Well, she has married and is currently Lady Pashley. Lord Chillingsworth is her brother."

"I will admit that he did seem much taken with our Emily," her mother said. She adjusted another bloom. "Do you know what he's worth?"

Emily glowered at her mother. "No. And it would be rude to inquire."

"I would ask his sister." This from Judith. "It isn't rude when you ask a friend."

"If this gentleman has taken a keen interest in you, Em, it would prudent to make a few inquiries about him," her father said, coming to his feet. "I won't have a fortune hunter chasing after my daughter."

"Lord Chillingsworth is not a fortune hunter." Emily followed her father out into the hall. "If he attends the theater, I will introduce him to you. You will see for yourself."

Her father halted and studied her face. "You like him."

Emily's face warmed under her father's perusal. "He is tolerable company."

Frost would have been amused by her bland description of their friendship. Last evening, Frost had lain between her bare legs and used his tongue in a manner that would likely cause her to blush every time she thought of it for the next twenty years.

Her father's smile faded. "Enjoy yourself, Em, but there is no reason to be hasty. Your sister—" He tilted his head to see if his wife was listening. Satisfied that she wasn't, he continued. "Lucy wasn't as sensible as you. Maybe if she had taken her time, not rushed into marriage with Leventhorpe, she would still be with us."

"Oh, Father," Emily whispered, impulsively embracing him. She was not the only one still grieving for her sister.

He patted her on the shoulder and stepped back. "Don't let your mother rush you into marriage. I want you to be happy."

Emily cleared her throat. "You have nothing to worry about. Lord Chillingsworth is just a friend."

"Good, that's good." He walked away from her. Without stopping he said, "I used to say the same thing about your mother."

Frost waited in the hotel lobby for his mother. What he had to say to her was best said in private, but he did not trust himself to be alone in the same room with her.

She froze when she saw him. The flash of fear in her eyes revealed she wasn't as stupid as he thought.

"Good afternoon, Mother," he said genially. He gestured for her to join him. "I hear you have decided not to leave England, after all. In fact, you have gone so far as to defy me by approaching my sister."

"Vincent," she began.

"Who did you think Regan would run straight to after you told your woeful tale about how you have been searching for a way back into your daughter's arms?"

"She was very upset with you."

Frost touched his cheek. "Aye, that she was, but don't worry about it. We have had our squabbles. You will be pleased to know that Regan and I managed to work things out."

His mother was troubled by the news.

"The risk you took is admirable," he continued in a conversational tone. "Since I was being difficult, you turned to Regan and her husband in the hope that I would pay you whatever amount you named to get you to leave. Very devious."

"I have not lied to you, Vincent. I was curious about Regan. I have often wondered if she looked like me—"

"She is nothing like you," he said cuttingly. He sat back and smiled. "Or me. However, I will admit that you have made an impression on her."

"You are upset that she no longer views you as a saint. Saint Vincent."

He laughed. "Madam, if you remain in town, you will learn that no one credits me as being a saint. Least of all Regan."

Frost stared at her until she began to fidget. "Good news! You will be pleased to know that I have changed my mind."

His mother brightened. "On the amount we discussed. I can give you the name—"

"It won't be necessary. I have decided that denying you access to Regan is petty. You want to be a part of your daughter's life, and Regan is pleased to have a mother again. I have come to welcome you to the family."

Frost stood and bowed. "I wish you well."

"Uh, wait . . . Vincent," she said, rising and chasing after him. He didn't halt until he had stepped outdoors. "There is the small matter of my expenses."

"Have the hotel send me your bills. I will settle the debt," he offered. "Is there anything else?"

"I need more than you settling my hotel bill, Vincent. I have other expenses."

"A difficult quandary to be certain." He took a deep breath to deliberate on the problem. "I see no reason why I cannot continue to pay your blackmail. Since you're back in the family, we'll just call it your annual allowance."

She grabbed him by the arm. "Damn you, I told you, it's not enough!"

Frost shook off her hand. "Then I suggest you learn to live within your means."

Chapter Twenty

Several days had slipped by before he had caught a glimpse of the elusive Miss Emily Cavell. Regan had told him that she had spoken to her at Lady Goodrick's fete on Tuesday. Sin and Juliana had enjoyed her company at Lord and Lady Damsell's late supper on the same evening. On Wednesday, Sophia and Isabel had introduced her to Lady Netherley. He was particularly distressed by this news, since the marchioness prided herself on being a successful matchmaker. The last thing he wanted was for Vane's elderly mother to get it in her head that she needed to find a husband for Emily.

There were numerous balls this evening, but no one had been able to tell him which one Emily would be attending. He had already searched two ballrooms; Lord and Lady Browett's residence was his third stop.

He swiftly paid his respects to his host and hostess, and moved on to finding the errant lady.

Frost noted he was not the only Lord of Vice in attendance. Vane and Isabel were chatting with Lady

Netherley and another woman. On the opposite side of the room, he saw Juliana, Sophia, and Reign. Juliana's husband wasn't with the small group, but he imagined Sin hadn't strayed far from his lady.

Frost raised his hand to acknowledge his friends. Reign beckoned him to join them. He headed in their direction but halted. Perhaps he should have a private word with Lady Netherley first.

"Lord Chillingsworth," a female voice called out, and he glanced over his shoulder to see Lady Gittens moving toward him.

Frost took her hand and formally bowed. She curtsied. "Lady Gittens, it is good to see you again. I pray you have been enjoying our good weather."

She opened her fan and gave him a coy look. "Is that why I have not seen you, my lord? Have you been hunting?"

"You know I cannot resist a challenging sport, my lady," Frost said, preparing to take his leave.

He did not wish to hurt the lady's feelings, but their brief affair was finished. The decision had been made even before he had met Emily. However, Lady Gittens was not quite ready to let him go, and situations like this often resulted in dramatic tantrums—something he preferred to avoid this evening.

"If it is sport you desire, perhaps we should adjourn to the back gardens, my lord."

Her meaning was clear, and there had been a time when he would have willingly followed her into the gardens or anyplace they could have stolen a few minutes to play their wicked games.

"I must regretfully decline, my lady."

It had been on the tip of his tongue to say, *Perhaps another time.* However, the simple creature would merely take him at his word.

Her face fell at his polite rejection. A gentleman accidentally bumped into her, giving her the opportunity to move closer.

"I wish you would reconsider," she said, stroking his arm. "My afternoons have not been the same without you, Frost."

Frost felt the stirrings of regret. He should have ended his relationship with the lady weeks earlier. "You will find someone else to amuse you, Maryann."

"Let's go upstairs," she coaxed. "Give me a chance to change your mind."

Frost didn't hear a single word. He had glanced over Lady Gittens's shoulder, and his gaze locked with Emily's. She was far enough away that she shouldn't have heard the widow's invitation, but her pained expression revealed that she had deduced he was speaking to one of his former lovers.

"Damn," he murmured, removing Lady Gittens's hand from his sleeve. "I must go."

"I—what?" The widow turned around to see the reason for Frost's abandonment, catching a glimpse of Emily as she walked away. Her eyes narrowed. "Who is she?"

Frost did not bother answering her. He had to find Emily before she thought the worst of him.

It was probably too late.

With her chin held high, Emily did not know where she was heading. She pushed her way through the crowd, needing to get away from all of these people—away from Frost.

Emily had not been introduced to the lady he had been speaking to, but there had been an air of familiarity between them. She saw how close they had stood with their heads bowed in a private conversation; the woman caressed his coat sleeve.

That woman had been his mistress.

Emily was certain of it. Tears were to be expected, but her eyes were dry. She was too furious to cry. As for her face, there was nothing to be done. Her pale complexion revealed too much; if she had any sense she would start spending more time in the sun to darken her skin.

"Emily!"

She stared blankly at the smiling brown-haired woman whom she had almost collided with. Emily had been so distracted by Frost and his mystery woman, it took her a moment to recall the name of a lady she had spoken to on several occasions.

Lady Vanewright. Isabel. She was the wife of one of Frost's friends. Another Lord of Vice. Her mouth trembled. She had to get out of this ballroom before she did something foolish.

"My apologies, Isabel. I cannot—I have to get away." Emily gulped. "There are too many people. Please."

The countess took one look at her face and simply said, "Come with me."

She took Emily's hand and together they made their way to one of the side doors that opened into a passageway. Guests and servants filled this area as well, but Isabel had another destination in mind. When she reached the stairs, she urged Emily to descend them.

"Earlier, I was looking for my husband and discovered this small room," she explained, opening the door. "We are in luck. It is still empty. The door over there leads to the library. Since most of the guests are upstairs, this is likely the quietest room in the house."

"Thank you." She was unsure if she should reveal anything else. "You should return to your husband. I will be fine."

Isabel hesitated, her brown eyes full of warmth and compassion. "Vane saw me leave with you. He will assume we left to find a quiet place to talk if I do not return to the ballroom. I can see that you are distressed. Is there something I can do? Can I get someone for you?"

Emily shook her head. "No. I just—I am being foolish."

"Is this about Frost?"

Startled, she gaped at the other woman. "How did you guess?"

Isabel pressed her lips together as if she was struggling not to laugh. "Well, it wasn't much of a guess. Vane and I saw Frost enter the ballroom. He didn't join us and he seemed distracted, as if he was looking for someone. We assumed it was you."

"Why me?" There were more than two hundred guests packed into that narrow ballroom. "And you are wrong. I was not the lady Frost was seeking."

"Oh no!" The countess seemed genuinely upset

on her behalf. "Though I suppose it isn't too surprising. After all, we are talking about Frost. Still, he seems genuinely fond of you. Even my husband had made a small wager with—" Isabel smiled, realizing she had said too much.

Before Emily could press the lady further, the door opened and the last man she wanted to see was standing in the doorway. He braced his hand on the frame of the door, looking slightly disheveled and out of breath.

"Isabel, your husband is looking for you."

A mutinous expression flashed across her delicate features. "Vane is aware that I am with Emily."

"Regardless, your husband is expecting you. Upstairs. Now." Frost stepped aside, clearing the threshold for the countess's departure. "I would hate to see that unblemished flesh marred with bruises."

Emily gasped, distressed by the thought that the lady might be punished because of her. "Maybe you should go. I will be fine."

Isabel glared at Frost. "Don't listen to him, Emily." She marched up to the earl. "My husband doesn't beat me."

Frost smiled benignly at her. "Well, maybe he should."

The countess glanced back at her. "I wish you luck, Emily. You're going to need it."

Chapter Twenty-one

Frost stared at Emily, attempting to deduce how angry she was at him. Would she try to run away from him? Grab the gold-and-black lacquer vase and throw it at his head? Or would she be provoked to violence, as his sister had been, and try to slap him? Would he even try to stop her, he wondered. He was not guilty of any wrongdoing. Nevertheless, his past sins were numerous, and often he had escaped any real punishment.

"I hope I was not interrupting anything important," he said politely, assuming the ladies had been discussing him. Isabel was a sweet-natured lady who seemed to like him well enough, but Frost was not counting on her to defend him.

Emily's mouth thinned with her obvious displeasure. "If you would stand aside, I will take my leave as well, my lord."

A gentleman would have done as she had asked. Instead he shut the door and locked it. He pocketed the key. "Not until we have had a chance to talk."

"I have nothing to say to you." Her sulky pout was endearing. "Now give me that key."

He parted his hands, palms forward, and offered her what he considered a disarming smile. "I must regretfully refuse. However, you are welcome to come closer and try to take it from me."

Fury flashed in her hazel eyes. Frost tensed, his muscles readying for her response. Emily ran toward the pier table that displayed the lacquer vase, and he had visions of blood and shattered porcelain. She managed to surprise him by veering to the right, which placed the sofa between them.

"Are we playing a game of chase, Emily?" he asked, not moving from his position at the door.

"No, I am getting away from you!"

Emily grabbed the front of her skirt and dashed to the side door at the far end of the room. She violently twisted the doorknob, only to discover that it was locked.

"A pity you don't have a key," he said blandly, walking toward her. "If you ask me nicely, I might give you mine."

"You disgust me."

"Of course, you could always pound on the door. Maybe someone will hear you on the other side," he helpfully suggested. Before she could act on it, he added, "Though the plan does come with some risks. Whoever opens the door will know you are alone in the room with me."

Frost caught her easily when she charged him. He laughed as he whirled her about, savoring the feel of her as she struggled in his arms.

"Give me that key!" she raged at him.

"No."

A sound of frustration escaped her lips as he spun her around and pushed her up against the nearest wall. As he had anticipated, Emily tried to slip her hands into his evening coat to retrieve the key, but he was stronger and quicker. He captured her wrists and pinned her arms over her head.

"Let me go!"

"I think not." He laughed as he used his hips to hold her in place. "This position gives me all sorts of ideas."

Emily stopped struggling, and the hurt look she gave him cut him in half. "Please. You are being cruel."

"And you, my green-eyed lady, are jealous."

The accusation brought her stubborn chin up. "I most certainly am not jealous."

"Truly? Then why did seeing me speaking to another lady send you running out of the Browetts' ballroom?" He had seen the confusion and the pain on her face before she had turned away.

"I walked out of the ballroom," she corrected. "There were too many people, and I sought a quiet refuge. Isabel decided to join me, having discovered this room earlier."

"Kiss me."

Her eyes widened in astonishment. "You expect me to kiss you?"

"If I misunderstood your hasty departure, then you should have no excuse not to kiss me." His hooded gaze dropped to her mouth. "The carnal liberties you granted me in your bedchamber have haunted me since our parting. Just one kiss. Prove you aren't vexed with me."

He lowered his head. She turned her face away.

"Ah, I see." He indulged himself by caressing her cheek with his lips. "So you *are* jealous."

Outraged by his accusation, she tilted back her head to deny the charge. "I am not—"

Frost kissed her. Firm and full of pent-up frustration, his mouth moved over hers possessively. Emily tried to keep her lips pressed together, but he was in no mood to be patient. Releasing her wrists, his right hand cupped her chin and coaxed her to open her mouth for him. His tongue laved her lower lip, slipping inside. Frost moaned. He half expected her to bite him, but after a minute she melted against him.

Emily gripped the upper sleeves of his evening coat and pulled him closer. Her tongue dueled against his until she was the one filling his mouth, a desperate claiming that made his cock swell with need. His hand moved from her throat to her breast.

Frost remembered how her puckered nipples tasted against his tongue. Since that night, his thoughts kept returning to perfection of her breasts as he cupped them in his hands, the firm flatness of her belly, and how she cried out in ecstasy when he pleasured her with his mouth. He had been wrong. One taste had not been enough.

The virginal Emily Cavell had left this greedy scoundrel hungry for more.

Forgetting once again to breathe, Emily ended their kiss so she could take a few breaths. "Oh, Frost."

"You have no reason to be jealous, Em," he murmured, kissing the corner of her mouth. "I only want you."

Emily lowered her gaze. "Is she your mistress?"

Frost hesitated, uncertain if she truly wanted the truth. Most women did not want to know the details of a lover's past, but Emily still had doubts about him. Lies would only damn him.

"Yes," he admitted, and he could feel her body stiffening, mentally shying away from him. She would have moved away from him if he had not caged her against the wall with his body. "Or rather she was. It was a brief affair, and I had already ended it before we met."

"Did you tell *her*?" Emily gave him a peevish look. "Ivy is less clingy."

Frost chuckled. "There is no need to be jealous, love. I have no desire to renew my friendship with the lady."

"I told you, I wasn't jealous." At his raised eyebrow, she loftily admitted, "I was concerned."

"Well, I will have to think of a way to distract you."

Emily let out a shriek of surprise when he whirled her around. She stumbled backward, and Frost caught her before she could fall, laying her gently on the sofa cushions.

He tugged off his gloves as he knelt beside her. He placed a hand on her ankle.

"Frost . . . no, you mustn't."

"You have a fondness for the word *no,*" he grumbled.

Frost was unused to a lady refusing his advances. Females of all ages adored him. He would never force himself on Emily, but he was not above applying a little persuasion.

"You have pretty ankles."

Emily giggled. "You should not be admiring my ankles."

"How can I resist such delicate bones? I want to put my mouth on them, nibble this particular spot . . . right here." Using his finger, he traced the indentation between her ankle bone and heel. "And then I would grow bolder."

"I do not believe that is possible, my lord."

"I would trail kisses up your finely formed calves." His hand slipped under her petticoat and possessively moved up her leg. "The back of your knees. Another spot worthy of my attentions."

"You must stop," she begged. "Someone might come."

If he continued, it might well be him. "Silly girl, the doors are locked, and I have the key."

Her lips curved into a sly smile. "Do you?"

Emily opened her hand, revealing the key.

She had managed to surprise him. "You naughty girl," he scolded, tickling her just above the knee and making her laugh. "You hoodwinked me."

"Yes," she said, sounding rather pleased with herself.

Frost found the notion very arousing. His cock always seemed to be aware of the lady. "Keep the key," he said generously as he found the long slit in her drawers. "Some locks need a delicate touch."

"Frost." She tried to glare at him, but she bit her lip at his touch.

"You're wet, Miss Cavell," he murmured, pleased by the discovery. She might have been vexed, but she still desired him. "Have you thought how it felt when I tasted the honey between your legs?"

"Not at all."

"Liar." He pressed his fingers against the opening of her sheath. His fingers sank into her. "There is no shame in liking my touch. I enjoyed giving you pleasure. Last night, when I was alone in my bed, I thought of the taste of you on my tongue while I touched myself."

"You shouldn't speak about—"

"Of what?" He slid a thumb up the damp slit between her legs and rubbed the sensitive nubbin. "Just thinking of you hardens my cock until it bursts with hot seed."

"It's unseemly," she protested, which ended in a low moan. "I shouldn't . . . you shouldn't be talking to me like this."

Frost kept stroking her, sensing the fever was building in her. Slick with her arousal, his fingers slipped deeper. "You should be pleased that you have so much power over me. That I worship you . . . would kill any man who tried to touch you."

Emily's eyes widened at his declaration. "I don't—there is no one else I—"

Before she could cry out, Frost covered his mouth with hers, drinking in her release. Her muffled sob brought him close to spilling his seed. He knew how to extend her pleasure, and his skilled, nimble fingers kneaded and stroked her drenched flesh as the sensitive muscles of her sheath pulsed against his hand.

With the scent of her release intoxicating him, Frost blindly reached for the buttons of his trousers. He needed to place his cock against her. The feel of her flesh against his would assuage the lust he was feeling. He could take care of himself later. Or maybe he could convince her to watch as he—

"Lord Chillingsworth, are you in there?"

Frost and Emily froze at the sound of Lady Gittens's voice. How had Maryann found him? He placed a finger to his lips as he gently removed his other hand from Emily's skirt. The poor girl was too embarrassed to protest. Her face was an alarming red, and he worried that she might faint. He helped her sit up and smoothed down her skirt.

"Persistent chit," he muttered, sending Emily an apologetic glance. "She must have followed me from the ballroom. This isn't my faul—"

Emily jumped up from the sofa and walked to the other side of the room. "You had better go," she said, her gaze as remote as her voice. "She obviously believes you and she are not—Just go."

With the scent of her on his hand, he tugged on his gloves. "Em . . ."

"Go," she fiercely whispered.

"I need the key."

Emily threw it at him. He caught it out of the air and sighed. Maryann had a lot to answer for. Never in his life had he regretted bedding a woman.

He marched over to Emily and kissed her hard on the mouth.

"We are not finished," he said, giving her a light shake to get her to meet his eyes. "I will escort Lady Gittens back to the ballroom so you can slip out unnoticed."

"Frost?"

Emily cast a stony look at the door. "Your Lady Gittens is waiting for you."

"She is not my—" He gave up. Emily was in no mood to listen to him. "We will discuss this matter later."

He headed for the door.

"If you find the time, pray give your former mistress my regards," she said cattily.

Frost winced, realizing that even sweet Emily had claws when she felt cornered. He glanced back, but she had turned her back on him. Muttering to himself, he jabbed the key into the lock and opened the door. He was through the narrow opening and had the door shut before the startled Maryann could glimpse the lady who had replaced her.

Chapter Twenty-two

"A moment if you please, Miss Cavell," Lord Leventhorpe said, catching her as she passed the library.

Emily curtsied and pasted a smile on her face for the man who had once been betrothed to her sister. "Good evening, my lord. I was not aware that you were in attendance this evening."

He bowed over her hand. "I had paid my respects to your parents earlier, but they had lost sight of you in the ballroom."

There was a slight censure to his inflection, though she could not understand why he would concern himself about her whereabouts.

"It is quite the crush," Emily said, dreading her return to the ballroom.

Frost had assured her that his relationship with Lady Gittens was over and done with, and she believed him. His expression had grown rather fierce when he heard the woman call out his name. Nevertheless, she had no desire to watch him and his former mistress together, even if he was cutting all ties with her.

Emily was also uncertain whether she wanted to see Frost. Every time he put his hands on her, he was pulling her deeper into his sensual web. The things he had done to her with his hands and mouth intrigued and frightened her.

With each encounter, she was finding it more difficult to resist him.

Lord Leventhorpe placed his hands behind his back as they strolled together. "I am pleased to see you again, Miss Cavell. Or may I call you Emily? After all, we were almost family."

"Of course. I would be honored if you called me Emily."

He offered her his arm, and she saw no reason to refuse him.

"Wonderful. Even though Lucy and I never married, I like to think of you as my younger sister. Or is that too forward?"

Emily thought of Frost pushing her down onto the sofa and slipping his hand under her skirt. "Forward?" she echoed. "Not at all. I know my parents think of you still as a member of our family."

"You honor me." They walked in silence for a few minutes before he spoke again. "Actually, I was planning to call on you this week. I hope you do not view me as indelicate, but I had a personal favor to ask of you."

"Me?" She could not imagine what Lord Leventhorpe might require from her. "How may I be of service?"

"It's about Lucy, Miss Cavell—uh, Emily." A look

of discomfort crossed his face. "I realize you were with her at the end."

"Yes."

"After her death, I assume you went through her belongings. Did you find any letters?"

Puzzled, she halted and stared at him. "Letters? What sort of letters?"

"Lucy was a beautiful woman. She was loved by all and had countless friends. I know she kept in touch with many of them when she was not residing in London. I thought you might have found them."

"I don't recall there being any letters, my lord," she replied with candor. "Why do you ask?"

He gave her a sheepish grin. "As the risk of making a fool of myself, I was hoping to read any letters that you might have found. Reading words that were meant for my beloved Lucy would bring me closer to her."

Emily had not realized Lord Leventhorpe was still in love with her sister.

"It doesn't make you foolish. I think it is rather sweet," she said. "If you wish, I could ask my mother about it. Perhaps she tucked them away somewhere."

Nodding, he patted her hand. "I would be in your debt, Emily. Thank you."

"My pleasure," she said, giving him a genuine smile.

"Are you returning to the ballroom?" At her nod, he continued, "I would be honored if you would be my partner in a dance of your choosing. If you have other plans, you do not have to accept—"

"Not at all," she said, relieved that she would not have to enter the ballroom alone. "I would love to dance with you."

Frost stalked into the ballroom in search of Emily. He had pulled Maryann aside and made it clear one again that their physical relationship had ended. While it had been enjoyable, he had no interest in pursuing her inside or outside the bedchamber. The widow had not taken it well. There had been copious amounts of tears and anger. The definitive parting had ended with a slap, because the furious woman knew another lady held his affections.

"You are a cold bastard, Chillingsworth. You are incapable of loving anyone," she had tearfully raged at him.

Frost did not argue with the woman. Maryann was angry, but he had not whispered pretty lies into her ear to get her into bed. She had entered their relationship with her eyes wide open, proclaiming that she was an enlightened woman who understood their arrangement was purely physical.

The spitting, embittered woman who had hurled curses at his head when she had taken her leave had fooled herself into believing that she loved him.

Frost regretted hurting her. He had liked her, enjoyed her company for a brief time, but only his cock had been truly engaged in their relationship.

He wondered if he could convince Emily to return downstairs to that small anteroom that connected to the library. He wanted to see her laughing up at him as he pressed her into the sofa and kissed her until she was breathless. After Maryann's unwelcome appearance, he doubted it, but he would settle for teasing her until she blushed.

The heat in the ballroom had increased during his absence. If not for Emily, he would have departed hours earlier. Frost casually walked the boundary of the large room in the hope of catching a glimpse of the lady. It wasn't until he reached the area that had been put aside for dancing that he noticed her. She had partnered with Lord Fothergill.

Didn't she have any sense? What was she doing dancing with that bounder? The man was also a terrible shot. Years ago, he had fought an infamous duel with Lord Quinton over a mistress. Quinton had lost part of his left ear because of the man's unsteady hand.

Frost took a step forward when Emily smiled at Fothergill.

"I recognize that particular look in your eye, and I wouldn't recommend it," Sin said, crossing his arms.

Together they observed Emily and Fothergill maneuver the lively steps of a country dance.

"I wasn't going to hurt him," Frost protested. *Much.* He shrugged. "At least, I would have allowed him to limp away."

"Fothergill isn't the only gent you have to worry about," his friend said, sounding as if he was struggling not to laugh. "During your absence from the ballroom, Miss Cavell has had a flock of suitors vying for a dance."

His vision dimmed as his eyes narrowed on the dancing couple. It took him a minute to recognize the emotion that was making his head pound. Jealousy. He was rarely inflicted with the sentiment, and he disliked it. He had teased Emily about her reaction toward his former mistress, and now he felt as if he owed her an apology.

Well, until she slipped away to flirt with other gentlemen.

"Who?"

Sin gave him an assessing glance, probably debating on whether he should give him the names. "Lord Leventhorpe, Lord Golland, Hunter's cousin—and if you ask, he will gladly throttle the gent for you—two young gentlemen who look young enough to make me feel old, and now Fothergill."

"Who were the lads?" Though Frost suspected he knew who had been sniffing around Emily.

"It was the twins. You know the ones. I don't recall their names," he said carelessly. "Frost, I am not the only one who has noticed that you have been behaving rather oddly. You seem distracted, easily provoked, and your interest in Miss Cavell is concerning your sister."

"Regan should pay more attention to the viper she has allowed into her life," Frost said, still unhappy with his mother's bid to reenter their lives. "As for Miss Cavell, the lady is no one's business but mine."

His friend did not immediately reply. Finally, he said, "She is unlike your usual conquests."

"You must be referring to her virginity," Frost said, amused that Sin would attempt to lecture him.

Before his marriage to Juliana, the marquess had carnal appetites that rivaled his own. And the man's fondness and clever uses for pearl necklaces were well known in certain circles. Frost would wager that several of the pearl necklaces he had noticed around the necks of many ladies this evening had been treasured keepsakes from Sin's wilder days.

"Don't fret about Miss Cavell." The dance with Fothergill had ended, and he was eager to approach her before she returned to her family. "She enjoys my company, and you know better than to suggest that I would hurt a lady."

He ruthlessly squelched any guilt he might have been feeling for Lady Gittens. The widow had known what she had been taking on when she had approached Frost. It was not his fault the lady had allowed her feelings to cloud over her sound judgment.

What he and Emily had was a different sort of friendship. Frost mentally shied away from defining it, but he could not think of another woman who baffled, infuriated, and drove him mad with lust all at once. She intrigued him so much he had been willing to break his rule about dallying with virgins.

"I know you wouldn't physically harm a woman, Frost," Sin said quietly. "Even so, there are other ways to hurt a lady like Miss Cavell. You are being selfish, and you know it."

He *was* being selfish.

Admittedly, he was flirting with danger by pursuing Emily Cavell. Her sister had uttered his name on her deathbed, which still troubled him. Lucy had been one of the few ladies he'd had no interest in bedding. It was just his rotten luck the lady was bedeviling him in death. Emily had assured him that she believed his avowals of innocence. Or at least she had until she had seen him with Maryann. Had her doubts returned? The notion that her trust might be conditional annoyed him, but he only had himself to blame.

Frost sensed the moment Emily had noticed him. She had been thanking that damn bounder Fothergill, and suddenly her gaze met his. Had she been aware of him all along? He wondered if she would stay or try to run from him again.

"Stay out of my business, Sin," he said lazily. "Our history and my love for you will not prevent me from breaking your nose."

"Stubborn arse," Sin muttered under his breath.

"Always."

Frost had lost interest in their conversation. He walked away to see if he could coax Emily into dancing with him.

Chapter Twenty-three

Emily was stunned when Frost casually sauntered up to her and bowed. She assumed he preferred to be discreet about their friendship, since there would be speculation about his intentions.

"Miss Cavell." He bowed low, lifting his gaze and captivating her with his turquoise-blue gaze. "You have collected a few admirers in my absence."

"Lord Chillingsworth," she replied, with a curtsy. "I see you have lost yours."

God willing, if there were other former lovers of his in the ballroom, they would have the good sense to keep their distance.

The orchestra played a waltz. Without asking, he swept her up into his arms and they began to dance. She had never danced with him, and yet they moved together as if they had waltzed countless times.

"You needn't worry about Lady Gittens," he said, moving with enviable grace. "Any hope of reconciliation has been dowsed, and the lady has departed on her own terms."

"So she slapped you."

"Hard enough to rattle my teeth," he conceded, revealing white perfect teeth. "Though I could scarcely complain."

"Indeed," Emily said, relishing his embrace as they danced. She felt the curious stares of various members of the *ton*. "We are being observed."

His eyebrow arched in feigned astonishment. "Does it bother you to be seen with me?"

Emily took a few seconds to think about it. "No. What about you?"

"Let them watch." He lowered his voice for her ears alone. "There is always speculation when I ask a lady to dance. After a while, it becomes tiresome, so I try to avoid it."

"And yet, here you are with me," she said, feeling ridiculously pleased that he would favor her with an unexpected boon.

No wonder his actions were fodder for the gossips.

"You will be the talk of the ball, my darling Emily," he teased. "Think how pleased your mother will be to have her drawing room filled to the rafters with gentleman callers."

The waltz ended too soon for Emily. She curtsied, and Frost bowed. Before she could escape, he took her by the hand and wrapped her fingers around his arm. "You cannot escape me so easily."

Frost had danced with her three times that evening. The knowledge that he had done something he normally avoided kept her spirits buoyant for the rest of the ball, and her good mood continued on the drive home. She had kissed her parents, ignoring their not-so-subtle curiosity about Lord Chillingsworth, and rushed upstairs to bed. When she fell asleep, she hoped that she would dream of him.

A few of the wives who were married to Frost's friends were not as charitable. Lord Sinclair's wife, Juliana, pointed out to Frost when they joined the couple that one dance would generate talk about his attentiveness toward Emily—three was flirting with scandal. He laughed and brushed aside the lady's concerns. No one could tell this man whom he could dance with or how many times.

Emily had never met anyone who seemed so indifferent to polite society's opinions and rules.

Frost can afford to be, Em. Can you?

She quashed and banished the traitorous thought. Frost found her amusing and challenging, and there was an attraction between them that neither one of them seemed willing to deny. He might not be in love with her, but he would never hurt her.

Emily finished plaiting her hair and crawled into bed. She should have been tired, but the evening had left her edgy. Restless. Reclining on top of the thick bedding, she idly stroked her right breast. Her nipples puckered in response. She had never given her body much thought. Bound in stays, undergarments, and layers of fabric, she had never thought to explore the pleasures of a light caress. Or considered what the dampness between her legs might mean.

Rolling onto her side, she slid off the bed and walked up the mahogany cheval mirror with a brass sconce attached to the spiral reed supports. Emily retrieved the candle from her dressing table and used it to light the two sconces so she could study her reflection. She returned the candle to the dressing table and stepped back.

How many times had she gazed into this mirror and not truly looked at her own body? She smoothed her nightgown, pressing the billowing fabric into her sides so she could see her waist. On a whim, she pulled the nightgown over her head and dropped it to the floor.

"Yes, much better," she murmured, tilting her head from side to side. What did Frost find so fascinating about her body? Her hand cupped her breast, testing the generous flesh. Well, not too much, she silently amended as she turned to the side so she could admire her stomach. She peered at the thick red curls between her legs.

Is it improper for me to touch myself?

Her hand slipped lower.

Frost had shown her things that were forbidden. In many ways, he knew her body better than she did. That seemed wrong. One day, she would marry and her husband would touch her as the earl had. How could she tell him what she liked or didn't like if she was ignorant of what brought her pleasure?

Emily was so distracted, she had not realized that she was not alone. Glancing beyond her reflection, she saw Frost standing behind her. She whirled around and placed one arm over her breasts, the other hand over her loins.

"What are you doing here?"

Frost calmly shut the door. "Thank God, you never

told your parents about the locks. I do not relish climbing through the window."

When he turned to lock her door, she crouched down and seized her nightgown from the floor. Emily held it in front of her.

"You can't stay," she whispered. "My family has retired for the evening."

"Trust me, I do not wish to disturb their sleep." He nodded at the mirror. "Charming backside, my lady."

Emily glanced back and gasped. She turned around to face the mirror and fell right into his plans. "Why are you here?"

Frost moved behind her, enfolding her into his embrace. He was aroused, she thought, as he teased by rubbing the front of his trousers against her buttocks.

She shivered delicately as he lowered his head and kissed her bare shoulder. "Turn around, and I will dress."

"What naughty things were you doing in front of the mirror, Emily?"

"Nothing," she swiftly denied. She observed him in the mirror while he placed his hand on her hip and pulled her against his front.

"You can tell me, sweet," he coaxed.

"I was curious. I have never looked at myself without my clothes."

He stilled. "Never?"

Emily shook her head. Uncomfortable, standing naked in front of him, she attempted to pull her nightgown over her head.

Frost plucked the garment from her hands and tossed it away.

"Give that back."

"No."

"You are impossible." She moved to retrieve it, but her midnight visitor had other plans. He spun her around so she faced the mirror again.

"It is a travesty that you have not gazed upon your delectable body," he whispered. He untied the ribbon at the base of her plaited hair. He combed his fingers through it until he was satisfied that it hung freely. "Beautiful."

"Frost." His name was a soft sigh on her lips. Emily marveled at the subtle changes in her body as he lightly caressed her. Her breasts tingled and her nipples became more pronounced. He swayed, his hand on her hip encouraging her to move with him. There was a slight pink coloring above her breasts. *Shame,* she told herself, but her body was not edging away from him. "No."

"Yes. You will like this, I promise." He nuzzled her neck with his lips, and the hidden flesh between her legs contracted. "Bring your hands to your breasts."

When she didn't immediately react to his order, he grabbed her wrists and brought her hands to her breasts.

"Cup them . . . feel the weight." He covered her hands with his. His thumbs caressed her nipples, and she shifted her stance.

His gaze burned like a blue flame in the candlelight.

She was very aware of the heat of his body. "Do you like them?"

"Aye, Emily." With his arms wrapped around her, he guided her hands over her breasts and down to her belly. "Have you touched your stomach?"

"Of course." He must have been observing her measure herself with her hands as she had admired her reflection.

"And lower . . . have you dared to touch yourself there?"

Frost moved her hand lower. With his hands covering hers, she could not pull away. Her hand skimmed over the nest of hair. It felt coarse, and the center of her was already damp. He tilted his head and pressed her fingers into the seam of the soft feminine folds of flesh between her legs.

What is the source of this wetness?

"Your body is preparing itself," he whispered into her ear.

He showed her how she could stroke and tease herself, and she was astounded by how good it felt.

Emily pressed her thighs together as she tried to resist the quivering sensation that had her body clenching. "What is my body preparing for?"

"Me" was his smug reply.

She slipped one of her hands free and reached behind to grab the rigid flesh beneath the front of his trousers. "What's this?" she asked.

"My cock," he said hoarsely; the teasing quality to his voice had disappeared. Her hand and buttocks rubbed against him, and he moaned in need, abruptly pulling her closer. "Christ, Emily. I need you. I told myself to stay away. I am not the man for you. It's madness."

Emily shifted, moving within his embrace until she faced him. "Would it help if I touched you?"

If she could ease his torment with a touch or a kiss, she could grant him this mercy. He had already given her so much pleasure, and her breasts tightened with anticipation as she reached for his cravat.

Frost squeezed his eyes shut. When he opened them, there was an intensity she did not understand. "My control is hanging by a thread, Emily. Be certain."

Emily was not certain of anything. However, she was curious about his body as he had been about hers. "Let me untie this," she murmured, concentrating on the intricate knot. A few minutes later, she tugged on the long length of cloth and dropped it on the floor.

Frost gave her a hard bruising kiss on the mouth.

Without another word, he began to undress. He peeled off his coat, while she helpfully unbuttoned his waistcoat. Both garments fell away. Next, his shirt. He pulled it over his head, revealing the hard, muscled planes of his chest.

Like a kitten, she rubbed her face against the dark hairs on his chest, and he groaned. She put her mouth on him and tasted the saltiness of his skin.

"You are killing me, love," he said, cupping her face and slowly kissing her.

When Frost touched her, she forgot to be embarrassed by her nakedness. His hand cupped her buttock and ground her pelvis against him.

"Tell me to stop, Emily."

Frost's hands were trembling, and it made her feel powerful. She shook her head. Her fingers reached for the side buttons on his trousers.

"No. Allow me." With his gaze locked on her face, he stepped out of his shoes and nudged them aside. Then he unfastened his trousers.

Emily's gaze lowered as his manhood was revealed. Darker than the rest of him, the long, thick flesh jutted out at her. He bent forward, concealing his manhood from her view as he shoved his trousers down his long hairy legs. His stockings were removed, and he was fully naked.

"You are beautiful," she whispered, admiring him as if he were a statue in the British Museum.

He looked as hard as marble, she thought, her gaze shifting back to the enthralling flesh between his legs. "May I touch you?"

Frost gritted his teeth. "Please." He took her hand and demonstrated how she could encircle the astonishingly heated flesh. "Squeeze."

His groan had her springing back. "Did I hurt you?"

Frost shook his head. "No. Do it again," he invited, pulling her toward the bed. He reclined against the mattress, and she joined him. Her fingers closed around his thick arousal, and she squeezed him again.

He groaned; the sound made her nipples ache. Below his manhood, she wondered about the hanging flesh at its base. "What is this?"

Before she could squeeze him there, Frost captured her hand and gave a dry chuckle. "It's very sensitive there. Be gentle. You may pet, but no squeezing."

He leaned back and allowed her to explore him as he had her. His body was so different from hers. Varied textures, muscle, the coarseness of the hair that covered his body. She assumed he tasted unlike her, and she leaned forward to put her mouth on his arousal.

"No." Instead he rolled her onto her back. "Another time. Too close. I have something else in mind." Frost moved between her legs, and she felt his manhood graze her inner thigh. He cupped the flesh between his legs, his expression one of pain.

Emily flinched at the first blunted touch of his manhood as he pressed against her damp feminine folds.

He reached down between them, and his fingers stroked her flesh before he parted her. "Breathe, Emily," he whispered into her ear.

His manhood slid deeper.

She tensed as he guided the head of his arousal, nudging until it found the source of her wetness. Frost gently tested the opening, bathing his rigid flesh and retreating.

"Christ, Emily, I need . . ." He closed his eyes and shook his head.

The pressure between her legs increased. It didn't hurt, but the fullness and sheer size of him overwhelmed her. His hips moved against hers. A slow dance, reminding her of a different kind of waltz. A carnal one.

Emily parted her thighs as she relaxed, savoring

the feel of him, but the shifting movement had her sheath taking more of him. His arousal, slick from her wetness, pushed deeper still, and she arched against him—then stiffened, the shock evident on her face when the fragile barrier that had been preventing him entrance gave way and he filled her completely.

"Frost?" She dug her nails into his upper arms.

He made soothing noises in an effort to calm her. "Does it hurt?" he murmured, kissing her slack mouth as she struggled to adjust to his invasion.

"Not precisely." The realization of what they had done was finally washing away the need she had for this man. "And my virginity?"

She already knew the answer, but she wanted him to confirm her suspicions.

"Gone," he said bluntly. He kissed her cheek. "I never intended to take it this far. I'm so damn sorry, Em."

"So what does that make me?" Emily whispered.

"Mine," he replied, just before he began to move within her.

He should have felt regret at a moment of carelessness, but he was honest enough with himself to accept that it was exactly what he had wanted from the beginning.

Frost had set out to seduce her, and the needs of his body had outweighed his common sense—and control.

He had taken her maidenhead.

Not intentionally. He could almost view it as fate.

Emily was not crying or cursing him. She was

probably bewildered at how quickly her innocence was lost and whether she was somehow different now that it was gone.

Frost withdrew his cock from her snug sheath, and her eyes widened in surprise.

"It gets better," he promised, thrusting deep. He repeated the action. Again and again. Until his back was slick with perspiration.

Afterward there would be time for sweet words and comfort, apologies, and possibly regret, though he doubted he was capable of that particular emotion when it came to her virginity.

He had never been interested in bedding a virgin, in being any lady's first lover.

Yet almost from the beginning, he had wanted to be Emily's first lover.

The realization snapped the final thread of his restraint. He groaned in despair as he blindly thrust against her, the release he could no longer hold back flooding into Emily.

She clutched him tightly as he shuddered helplessly in her arms, giving in what had begun as an act of taking.

Emily was his, he thought with fierce satisfaction.

As the heat of passion waned, he realized that such a claiming was not one-sided.

Whether she was prepared to accept it, he belonged to her.

Chapter Twenty-four

Emily could do little more than hold Frost as he buried his face against the side of her neck and shuddered. The heat rolling off his body suffused her as she felt the hot pulses of his seed fill her. Her body fluttered in response, reminding her of the stronger sensations he had created within her using his mouth and fingers. She felt little discomfort, but the growing awareness of what they had done brought a sharp pain to her heart.

Frost appeared to be equally nonplussed by their lovemaking. "Christ!" he said, lifting his head and meeting her overly bright gaze. "Emily . . . I—"

"Could you please—" Emily began, unable to vocalize her desire for him to get off her. She pushed at his chest. "I need—I cannot breathe."

And I need for you to go away.

Frost was still aroused, the thick, rigid length stretching her and making her all too aware of him. He stared down at her with an enigmatic expression on his face. On a muttered oath, he carefully withdrew from her. In a belated gesture of modesty, he grabbed the edge of the sheet to pull it over them, but Emily abruptly sat up. She offered him a generous view of her back as she allowed her legs to dangle over the side of the mattress.

She shut her eyes when he tentatively touched her on the back.

"Forgive me." Frost slipped his arms around her as he pulled her closer, until her backside was pressed against his manhood. His chin lightly rested against the dip between her neck and shoulder. "There is a reason why I do not involve myself with innocents, but all my good intentions seem to vanish whenever you are within reach. I hurt you. It could not be helped, but it is the only part of this night that I regret."

Emily stared off in the distance, trying to put words to her feelings. How could she feel joy and sadness at once? It would have been simpler if she could blame Frost for stealing her innocence. However, she had enjoyed his kisses and slow, teasing caresses. It had hurt when he had breached her maidenhead, but there were aspects of his lovemaking that she had enjoyed.

Holding him while he found completion within her had been an intoxicating experience filling her with a decidedly feminine power she had been unaware that she could possess.

"You are too quiet." He nipped her shoulder with his teeth. "That worries me."

Emily wrinkled her nose at his attempt at humor. "I was thinking that for a ruined lady, I don't feel much different."

She was a bit sore, but refrained from mentioning that particular detail to him.

"What's this?" He shifted her in his embrace. "You're not ruined."

"Of course I am," Emily said, the exasperation in her voice giving it a slight edge. "The path of a lady's ruination is at the hands of a scoundrel." She frowned and glanced below his waist. "Well, not precisely your hands. It was your—"

"Enough," Frost said, cutting her off. "Let me be clear. You are not a ruined lady because you surrendered your maidenhead. In the first place, no one evens knows we have become lovers. And second, I have no desire to share the delightful news in the *Morning Post*."

Her lower lip jutted out mutinously when he refused to take her seriously. "And what would be that good news, Lord Chillingsworth?"

Frost groaned. "This is about Lucy again, is it not?" When her lips parted, he immediately assumed that old doubts about his connection to her sister had resurfaced, and the leash on his temper snapped. "Have I mentioned how damn infuriating it is to be accused of seducing your sister, when the only Miss Cavell I have bedded is you!"

"I believe you," she said, sounding equally exasperated. That seemed to mollify him. "And I wasn't accusing *you*. Though there was little doubt in my mind that Lucy had a lover that was someone other than Lord Leventhorpe."

Frost stroked her jawline. "You might never learn the gent's name. Your sister had a look about her that caught a man's eye. However, you are allowing your guilt to blind you to a few undeniable facts. Lucy was not a paragon. Like you, she was spirited. She was also a vain and needy woman who tried to manipulate those around her to assuage her selfish whims."

She did not like anyone speaking ill of her sister. "Oh, really? And how were you immune to her charms?"

"Contrary to the rumors"—he laughed—"and my eagerness to lay claim to your delectable body this evening, I do not bed every wench who flirts with me."

Emily gasped when Frost suddenly pushed her onto her back and pinned her to the mattress with his body.

"I never flirted with you!"

"It would be ungentlemanly to call you a liar." He kissed her left breast. "Granted, you had good reason to resist me. Just as I tried not to fall prey to your innocent wiles."

Frost was being outrageous. "Let me up."

He bit her earlobe and she shivered. "Shall I tell you why I was never inclined to pursue your sister?"

Emily nodded, wholly aware that Frost's hand was moving lower. "Why?"

"Her beauty paled in comparison to yours." His wicked grin revealed that she was over her head with this man. "If anyone is ruined, it is I, sweet Emily. Shall I prove it? I promise I will be gentle."

Emily closed her eyes, trusting Frost to be a man of his word.

Frost was whistling a merry tune as he entered Nox. He credited his high spirits to the past four hours he had spent in Emily's bed. Although she had been too tender for prolonged lovemaking, he had demonstrated that there were other ways to pleasure a lady. Emily had barely acknowledged him when he reluctantly slipped from her bedchamber.

Instead of heading for the public rooms, Frost climbed the stairs to the Lords of Vice's private rooms. Berus was usually waiting to greet him and his friends, but the hour was late. Using his key, he unlocked the door and headed for the large saloon. He could not hazard a guess as to how many evenings he and his friends had sought various amusements in this room. The billiards table, in particular, was one of his favorite indulgences. He idly wondered if he could persuade Emily to join him at Nox for a game or two.

Frost's intriguing fantasy vanished at the sight of Berus sitting in one of the chairs; Dare, Vane, and Hunter hovered over him with worried expressions on their faces.

"What the hell happened?" Frost demanded when he noticed the steward was holding several bloody handkerchiefs against his nose.

Sin entered the room from another connecting door with a glass of brandy in his hand. "Better late than never," he said to Frost. "I was beginning to think you hadn't received my message."

"I didn't. If you called a meeting, where are Saint and Reign?"

"Downstairs talking to the police," Dare replied.

Frost strode to Berus and knelt at the older man's side. In some ways, the man was the closest thing he had to a father. "Let me see," he asked, taking matters into his own hands by peeking under the bloody linen.

He cursed fluently.

Someone had done an adequate job using his fists on Berus's face. His nose was broken; there was swelling and a cut under his right eye; his lower lip was twice its normal size and still bleeding; and there was dark bruise forming on the man's forehead.

"That cut looks bad. It might need a stitch or two," Frost announced, though he assumed his friends had come to a similar conclusion. "Has a surgeon been summoned?"

"I don't need a surgeon," muttered Berus.

"Aye, I sent one of the servants to rouse one from his bed," Sin said, his eyes simmering with rage. "Vane, why don't you see if the man has arrived downstairs?"

Vane gave Frost a troubled glance as he walked away to see to his task.

Everyone was tense and grim, and no one was bothering to explain why their steward was trying not to bleed on the carpet. "Does anyone want to tell me what happened?"

Although they tried to run a respectable establishment, there was always an element of danger when volatile tempers, liquor, and gambling losses were part of the nightly entertainment. This evening would not have been the first time that the man had been forced to confront an intoxicated patron.

"It was Halward," Berus said, his voice distorted by his swollen mouth.

"Someone let him into Nox," Frost asked in disbelief.

The steward shook his head. "I was lured outside. Someone had set a small fire with brush and rags, and I was worried about the club. I never anticipated it was a trap."

"The bastard hired pugilists to do his dirty work," Sin said, the harshness in his voice like a lash. "They dragged Berus away from Nox into the shadows and beat him senseless. One of the patrons found him crawling toward the street."

"This was a message directed to the Lords of Vice," Hunter said, his fingers digging into the back of the chair. His knuckles looked almost white. "Halward wants Nox or at least monetary bribes to keep his bruisers away."

"I say, let him try," Frost said, preparing to defend the club, even if it meant spilling his own blood. "Halward might feel differently if we paid him a visit."

"May I speak to you in private?" Sin interjected.

Without waiting for a response the marquess stalked out of the room. Frost patted Berus's shoulder, noticing that Vane had arrived with the surgeon. "Ah, the good surgeon will patch you up nicely.

With luck, any scars will make you more appealing to the ladies."

The steward smiled, and then winced in pain. Berus waved him off.

Frost stood and followed his friend through the door he had exited. He found Sin in the passageway that led to numerous bedchambers he and his friends had used when they were too deep in their cups to find their way home. The bedchambers had also been used for trysts with countless females since they had opened Nox's doors.

"You're worried about Berus," Frost said, noting his friend's thunderous expression. "He's been roughed up, but he's tough. A few days in bed and he will be fine."

"This isn't about Berus," Sin muttered. He braced his hand against one of the walls and stared at Frost. "Have you ever considered that this attack on Berus might be a sign that it's time to close Nox?"

"No," Frost said stubbornly. "Nox belongs to the Lords of Vice. Why would you even contemplate surrendering to that sniveling coward? Halward is a bully, but he's nothing without his hired muscle. He's no match for us."

"So this is what it has come to? Us . . . battling criminals?" Sin glared at him in anger and incredulity. "Have you thought above your own damn selfish needs? We have wives and children, Frost. People who depend on us to not *die* because we allowed our tempers and pride to cloud our judgment."

Sin's accusation stung. "I am not a fool. Nor am I suggesting we carelessly toss away our lives. Nevertheless, I never thought you would blithely hand over Nox to our enemies without a fight."

"Frost," Sin said wearily. "There are other ways to battle Halward. Legal ways that don't involve our people getting almost beaten to death in the streets."

Frost sneered. "Marriage has made you soft. Six years ago, you would have fought at my side without asking. You would have cut down any man who suggested that you close Nox." He shook his head in disgust. "I am finished with this conversation."

"Frost!"

He stepped back into the saloon, and it was apparent that his chat with Sin had not been so private.

"Do you all feel the same way?" He threaded his fingers through his hair and stared defiantly at them. "Are you prepared to close Nox because of the danger Halward poses?"

Their silence was damning.

"Well, then." A cynical smile twisted his mouth. "It heartens me to know that I can count on my friends. Enjoy the rest of your evening, gents."

Frost stalked out the door.

The sun had already risen when Emily woke. She was alone. Glancing about the bedchamber, she saw no sign of Frost's midnight visit.

She sat up and winced.

Dressed in her nightgown, her hand absently covering the tender flesh between her legs, Emily recalled how Frost had taken a dampened cloth and gently washed away the sticky evidence of their lovemaking. She had expected a little blood, some proof that her maidenhead was gone. However, Frost was too skilled as a lover to permit her to suffer. While his claiming had hurt initially, her body had swiftly embraced his manhood, anointing the unyielding flesh with her wetness as he filled her with his seed.

Her breasts tightened at the thought.

Frost had thoroughly ravished her, and she wondered when he would come to her again.

Emily pulled back the sheet, and a piece of paper fluttered to the floor. She climbed down from the bed to retrieve it.

No regrets.

Emily stared down at the words Frost had hastily scrawled. Was he expressing his own feelings or telling her not to feel guilty that she had enjoyed his lovemaking?

She smiled as she walked to her dressing table and slipped his note into a small drawer. Knowing Frost, he was probably ordering her to accept that last night had altered their relationship.

Since her maid had not entered to wake her, Emily assumed it was still early for her family to have awakened. Instead of ringing for Mercy, she slipped out of her bedchamber and walked down the hall to Lucy's old bedchamber.

Frost's note reminded her of Lord Leventhorpe's request for any letters his beloved Lucy might have left behind. With her family asleep, this would be the best time to search for them.

The last time Emily had entered the room, she had discovered her dying sister collapsed on the floor.

The unhappy memories had kept her from returning. She turned the doorknob, and the door opened. No one had locked the bedchamber.

Emily entered the shadowed interior and walked to the window. Opening the curtains, she noticed that the maids had kept the bedchamber prepared for guests. The room was spotless, and she felt a sharp pain in her heart at the realization that there was no evidence Lucy had ever slept here.

Or that she had died here.

Emily noted the rug had been replaced, but everything else was the same. She crossed her arms over her chest as she glanced at the furniture, wondering if her mother had removed all of Lucy's belongings from the room.

A quick search of her sister's dressing table and the table near her bed had her lips thinning in frustration.

Come on, Lucy . . . where would you have kept letters that had special meaning for you?

Emily searched the empty wardrobe and an old chest, looked under the bed, even checked under the cushions. Maybe she was searching for something that her mother had already found and packed away. If so, she would approach her mother after breakfast on Lord Leventhorpe's behalf. The woman had a soft spot for the man who should have been her son-in-law. She suspected her mother would give him any letters that had been tucked away.

She gave Lucy's bed a passing glance as she walked by. There was no doubt that her sister had had a lover.

Lucy was no paragon.

Frost's observation echoed in Emily's head. She had not wanted to listen. Defending her sister had become as instinctive as breathing. However, he was correct. Lucy had kept secrets from her family.

If Frost was not her lover, then who had sired her child?

Emily returned to the dressing table. She opened each small drawer, but all of them were empty. Frustrated, she tugged hard on the last one and managed to pull it free from its frame. She knelt down to reinsert it, and that's when she noticed the piece of paper wedged into the back.

"So Lucy had kept her letters in the dressing table," she murmured out loud.

Emily set the letter aside while she dealt with the drawer. Picking up the letter, she opened it and saw the salutation.

My dearest love . . .

This wasn't a letter from a friend, she thought, as she continued reading. When she had finished, it was abundantly clear that she owed Frost a sincere apology. She was holding proof that another gentleman had fallen in love with her sister.

Emily folded the letter. She could not share this letter with Lord Leventhorpe. He believed Lucy had been faithful to him, and she refused to steal that from him. There was no reason to disparage her sister's memory.

With the letter clutched in her hand, she returned to her bedchamber. Like Lucy before her, Emily hid her sister's letter so no one would find it.

She needed to speak with Frost. Perhaps he could help her uncover the answer to her most pressing question.

Who the devil is Captain Gladish?

Chapter Twenty-five

Unlike Frost who seemed to visit her whenever it suited him, Emily could not work up the nerve to visit him at his residence. It seemed unseemly for an unmarried lady to call on a gentleman. She thought about approaching Regan and asking for her assistance. However, that plan was flawed as well. Her friend's natural curiosity about Emily's relationship with Frost would place her in a difficult position. She did not wish to lie to Regan, but was not prepared to explain her complicated fascination with the lady's older brother.

Or if there was a possible future with the gentleman.

Perhaps it did not bode well that he preferred to keep their relationship private, though he did seem to enjoy taunting the gossips with his mischief, as when he'd danced with her more than once. Emily could not help but wonder if Frost had ever courted a lady in earnest. Probably not. Though to be fair, she conceded that no other gentleman had courted her affections so she was in no position to judge.

Her sister's expectations and her lover's failings

had led poor Lucy down a path of despair. Emily refused to make the same mistake.

Love and friendship were to be cherished. What she shared with Frost might not last, but she refused to waste the time she'd had with him on recriminations and regret. It was an enlightened approach, she reflected. Gentlemen who refused to be tamed by convention were wary creatures.

Instead of seeking out Frost, she chose to bide her time and wait for him to come to her. To ensure that he had no difficulty finding her, she had accepted Sin and Juliana's invitation to join them in their theater box. Other familiar faces greeted her as she took her seat beside the couple. Regan and Dare were present, and Isabel and her husband, Vane, arrived shortly after her.

Oberon, or The Elf King's Oath was a three-act opera that she had been looking forward to all day. Exotic locales, fairies, and young lovers—the tale appealed to her romantic heart, and she confessed as much to her new friends.

Regan laughed. "Reside in London long enough, and you will discover that no one attends the theater for the announced performance," she teased.

"Then why attend at all?" Emily asked.

Dare appeared equally amused. "The members of the *ton* wish to be admired and envied. It is the minor dramas that take place in the theater boxes that tend to be discussed long after the performances on the stage."

Dare and Regan exchanged intimate glances, as

if there was something that the couple was not telling her.

"Well, I can enjoy both," she assured them. She leaned closer to Regan so she did not have to raise her voice. "Will your brother be in attendance this evening?"

Overhearing her question, Sin's gaze was speculative when he said, "It is doubtful, Miss Cavell. Last evening, we had trouble at Nox and there was some disagreement on how it should be handled."

Dare and Vane seemed to tense at the marquess's vague explanation, which heightened Emily's concern.

"Trouble?" Emily brought her hand to her heart at the thought of Frost being hurt. "Was . . . was Lord Chillingsworth attacked?"

"Would it upset you if he had been?" Sin countered instead of offering an answer to her question.

"Frost is fine, Emily," Regan said, placing her hand on Emily's arm to draw her gaze away from Sin. "Truly. It was Nox's steward who was attacked. He—"

"Let's not give Miss Cavell further reason to level charges at why Nox should be closed," Vane drawled.

Although he was not precisely rude, his wife rapped his hand with her closed fan.

"That is enough," Isabel warned. "All of you are too upset about Berus to comprehend that Emily's interest has nothing to do with Nox."

Emily's blushing response concealed little from the three gentlemen. Of course Frost had told them of the comments she had made about seeing the end of clubs like Nox.

"I—you could not possibly believe I had anything to do with your steward's attack?" Emily stammered.

She had been in bed with Frost, though nothing short of torture would pry the admission from her lips.

"Not directly," Sin said, staring at her through a hooded gaze. "However, if I were you, I would choose my friends carefully, Miss Cavell."

"Not you, too," Juliana said, shaking her head. "You are spoiling for a fight, and Emily is not your adversary. If you get us tossed from the theater, you will be sleeping on the library sofa for the rest of the month."

Juliana was attempting to lighten the tension in the private box, but Emily belatedly realized that she had been invited to join them for not-so-pleasant reasons.

The Lords of Vice thought she might have something to do with the incident at Nox. Had Frost come to the same conclusion?

Her throat constricted as she rose from her seat. She could do little about the shame scalding her cheeks. "Pray excuse me, I am feeling a little light-headed from the heat. I believe I will take some air in the saloon before the opera begins."

Regan, Juliana, and Isabel also began to stand.

"We will join you," Regan said, glaring at the men.

"No." Emily wanted to be alone. If the ladies joined her, she would give in to her tears. "There is no need. I will not be long."

No one tried to stop her, and Emily was grateful.

She could have remained in the small private anteroom just beyond the curtain of the theater box, but she wanted to distance herself from Frost's friends. Emily did not attempt to deceive herself into believing that Regan would take her side if given the choice between her and the Lords of Vice. These gentlemen were part of Regan's family.

She did not really fit in their world.

Although it was tempting to head for the entrance and find a hackney coach to drive her home, Emily took the passageway that would open into the large saloon. There was no privacy, but the public room would help her keep her emotions leashed.

"Miss Cavell?"

Emily nearly stumbled, but she managed to catch herself in time. She turned to address the woman, and realized with growing dismay that she recognized her.

It was Frost's former mistress.

She could not imagine the evening getting any worse.

Chapter Twenty-six

Frost had kept his distance from Emily.

His friends' ridiculous assumptions that she might have been indirectly responsible for Halward's actions and Lady Gittens's daring confrontation at the theater had put a fine edge to his mood.

Emily was upset, and beyond his assurances and charm.

Instead of sulking or staining his fists with Sin's blood, Frost had chosen a different strategy to thaw Emily's icy reserve.

Frost had found her sister's Captain Gladish.

The man was residing just outside London. Frost had already sent one of his servants to the Cavell residence with a polite invitation for Emily to join him on a drive into the country. He would wager everything he owned that no matter how vexed Emily was at him, she would not decline his invitation.

His butler appeared in the doorway. "Lord Chillingsworth, you have a visitor. Are you receiving callers this afternoon?"

Frost admired his reflection as his valet stepped out of view. In her eagerness, had Emily come to him?

"Is it Miss Cavell?"

"No, milord, it is your mother." The butler appeared aggrieved. "As always, the lady is most insistent."

He had no time for or interest in seeing his mother. However, like the broken tip of a thorn buried in his flesh, she would fester and torment until he made the effort to dig her out.

"Escort her to the library. You have my permission to ignore all requests. My mother won't be staying long enough for you to carry them out."

Emily fussed with her bonnet for the fourth time as she and Frost traveled northeast of London to call on Captain Gladish. She could not decide if it was Frost's proximity or her impending meeting with the man who was possibly Lucy's lover that had her nerves just beneath her skin itching like a rash.

"You look fine," Frost drawled. "Your fidgeting is disturbing my nap."

Emily cast a side glance at her companion. His eyes were closed, and for most of their journey she did not think he was paying attention to her.

"I cannot believe you found Captain Gladish so quickly," she admitted, her hands settling onto her lap. "When I mentioned the letter a few days ago, I thought the search might take years."

"I had some incentive," he murmured.

Bewildered, she asked, "Good heavens, what could possibly be an incentive for you?"

Frost opened his eyes. She felt the impact of his

turquoise-blue gaze down to her toes. "You. View it as an apology, if you like."

He had mistaken her silence for anger, she deduced. Emily could not deny that she had been upset the night she had encountered Lady Gittens at the theater. However, she did not blame him for the lady's actions. He hadn't lied when he had told her that he had ended the affair.

"You don't owe me an apology about Lady Gittens," she said with a sigh. "She is a troubled woman, who believes she is in love with you."

Frost grimaced as he stretched. "Maryann understood the rules. More to the point, she doesn't love me. She merely thinks that she does."

The only rules he valued were his own. "Whether she does or not is unimportant," she said coolly. "The lady believes her affections are genuine. Dismissing them does not make her pain any less real."

"Emily," he began.

"We have arrived," she said, peering through the glass. "You mentioned that Captain Gladish is residing at his sister's house."

Emily pretended not to notice the look of frustration that darkened his expression. Frost was reluctant to let the matter drop, but she had given him little choice.

"Aye, let's go introduce ourselves to Lucy's captain."

The confusion on the man's face was to be expected. They had appeared on his doorstep without warning, and there was recognition in his gaze the moment his gaze settled on Emily.

"You must be one of Lucy's sisters," Captain Gladish blurted out before a proper introduction could be made. "Is Lucy here?" His gaze moved past them to their coach as if he expected Emily's sister to stick her head out the window to wave at him.

Was the fellow daft?

Emily must have had similar concerns before she edged closer to him. Frost longed to place his arm around her, but he did not want to press his luck.

"Perhaps we should speak in private," Frost said, unused to being the sensible one in the room. Or in this instance, the front hall.

Captain Gladish, who for a man who had to be in his early thirties had managed to hold on to his boyish looks, nodded and invited them upstairs to the drawing room.

They were offered tea, but Frost and Emily politely declined.

"Captain Gladish," Emily began once they were seated. "When was the last time you saw my sister?"

The earlier delight at the prospect of seeing Lucy had faded into wariness. Frost did not blame the man. The news they brought was going to alter his world, and not for the better.

"A little more than five years ago, I believe. Has something happened?"

"Yes." Emily reached into her reticule and pulled out the letter she had discovered in Lucy's bedchamber. "I assume my sister hid this because . . . well, I do not wish to be indelicate, but your letter makes your feelings quite clear. You were in love with a lady who was betrothed to another gentleman."

Captain Gladish accepted the letter Emily had offered him. Frost noticed the tremor in the man's hands as he unfolded the letter and skimmed his own words.

"Miss Cavell, you speak as if my love for your sister is in the past. I regret this is not so. A day hasn't passed when I have not thought of her and prayed for her well-being, even knowing that she chose to marry another man instead of me."

Emily glanced at Frost, her distress so obvious that he did not give a damn about appearances. He clasped her hand and slipped his other arm around her waist.

"Captain Gladish, I cannot tell you how much I loathe being the one to tell you. My sister did not abandon you because she had married another gentleman," she said, her voice cracking with sorrow.

Frost tightened his embrace, silently reminding her that she was not alone.

Anguish suffused the captain's face. "I beg of you, do not say it."

Emily retrieved her handkerchief and wiped the tears on her cheeks. "Lucy is dead, Captain Gladish. A little more than five years ago, she took her own life."

"My God, I have killed her," the man said starkly.

Moved by the captain's genuine grief, Emily shook her head. "How could that be? You were not even aware—"

Captain Gladish's face hardened. "Five years ago, Miss Cavell, your sister had accepted my marriage proposal. She was planning to end her betrothal. We were to marry, and she would have joined me on my next voyage. A fortnight passed, and she did not return to me. I wrote her several letters, but all of them remained unanswered. While I was at sea, I had come to the conclusion that Lucy had decided not to break her betrothal but lacked the courage to put her decision in a letter. All of these years . . . she was dead and I never knew."

Captain Gladish brought his arm to his face and openly wept.

Emily buried her face into Frost's shoulder and sobbed. The drawing room was thick with grief as the two people who loved Lucy the most were united in sorrow.

Frost's throat tightened in sympathy for what Gladish had lost. Emily had been seeking the man who had seduced and abandoned her beloved sister. She had not considered that Lucy had been capable of abandoning the hardworking sea captain who had simply loved her.

"You never told him about his unborn child," Frost said, thirty minutes later.

Emily's tears had dried, or maybe she had shed so many on behalf of Lucy she had nothing left inside her.

"How could I? For five years, Captain Gladish has continued on with his life believing the most honorable thing he could do for the woman he loved was to let her marry another man. I devastated him by revealing that my sister preferred death instead of fighting for their life together. It would have been too cruel for him to learn that she took the life of his unborn child as well."

Frost felt helpless. "I'm so sorry, Emily."

In an absent gesture, she dabbed the already damp handkerchief to her cheek. "I owe you an apology as well. I was so wrong—about you, the captain, even Lucy. I feel like such a fool."

"It wasn't your fault." He reached out to touch her, but she slapped his hand away.

"Stop the coach."

Startled, he stared at her. "Now?"

"Yes, stop the coach." Emily staggered forward to reach the small trapdoor in the roof. She pounded on the door until the coachman opened it. "Please stop the coach. I need to—please!"

The coachman brought the team to a halt, but Emily was impatient to leave her confines. Without waiting for the coachman to disembark, she flung the door open and almost fell to her knees in her haste to escape.

"Emily!" Frost roared as she raced away from him and the coach. He jumped down and shouted over his shoulder to the coachman, "I'll go after her."

She had disappeared into the tall grass, but her trail was easy for him to follow. They were far enough from the road that he could no longer see the coach, but that was not a concern.

Frost was worried for Emily. The captain had suffered a severe blow learning that the lady he still loved was dead. Emily was also hurt, and his longing to ease her sorrow warred with his rising need to throttle her long-dead sister.

He caught her by the arm and whirled her around to enfold her into his embrace. "Emily, you are going to make yourself sick if you continue."

"Oh, my God, Frost," she sobbed against his chest. "It hurts so much. I have kept Lucy's secrets for so long. I don't know what to do. Tell me what to do."

Guided by instinct, he tilted her head back and said, "You need to purge the poison and grief." He kissed her roughly, and he felt the sharp edges of her teeth cut into his lip. "Let it out. Use me. Share it with me."

Frost kissed her again, willing her to respond to the wildness rising within him.

Emily froze at his rough handling, and then suddenly she was blindly pulling at his coat. His hat went tumbling to the ground and her fingers were tearing at his hair as she kissed him with a fierceness that hardened his cock and filled him with unquenchable lust. Without releasing her mouth, he peeled out of his frock coat and let it drop to the ground.

"Christ, Em, I have to have you!" he growled against her mouth as his eyes darted from side to side for a suitable place to take her.

"Here," she panted as she kissed him again. "Now! I cannot wait."

Frost groaned as desire overruled common sense.

Emily had wrapped herself around him, limiting his ability to move, but he did not want to release her. So he merely dropped to his knees, pulling her to the ground with him.

"I don't want to hurt you," he said, lifting the front of her skirts above her knees.

She grabbed the front of his trousers at the waist, tugging until the buttons popped free from the eyelets. "You won't. Nothing matters. I need—"

Emily could not articulate what she wanted from him, but Frost understood the emotions roiling inside her. She was hurting, lost, and seeking the blissful oblivion passion could provide.

What he could give her.

Frost freed his fully aroused cock, grabbed the front of her drawers, and widened the slit in the linen with a single tug. This was no gentle claiming. Nor was one necessary. He pushed the head of his cock against her sheath and slid inside her.

Emily was as aroused as he was.

Her next words confirmed it. "More," she begged, arching against him.

Frost withdrew slightly so he could thrust into her wholly. She gasped and pulled his head down until their mouths met.

"I need you."

The three words unleashed what little control he had left to offer her. Cupping her buttocks, he pounded his cock into her drenched sheath with a wild abandonment that Emily seemed to embrace. She wrapped her legs around him, silently demanding that he drive himself so deeply she could no longer distinguish where he ended and she began.

He bit her on the shoulder, more than willing to fuck her senseless. Their fierce, desperate rhythm only put an edge to his hunger. Frost wanted to take her in other positions. Heedless of the flattened grass and dirt, he wanted to flip her onto her knees and take her from behind. He wanted to roll onto his back and make her watch as his cock slid into her. He needed to feel her mouth on him, to coax her to take him deeply into her throat and pump into her until she was swallowing his seed.

Emily arched against him and cried out. Her release gripped him by the balls, and he joined her. His groans of pleasure mingled with hers as her muscled sheath milked him of his seed. He held her tightly, pushing cock deeper. He wondered if a man could die from the exquisite pleasure of pumping his seed into a woman's womb.

If so, he would perish with a smug grin on his face.

Neither one of them spoke. He held her close as he listened to their labored breathing. His cock twitched inside her. He should have been sated, but the damn thing wanted more.

More of Emily.

If he had any sense, he should be worried.

But that was the problem with the stubborn, passionate woman in his arms.

He never seemed to get enough of her.

Chapter Twenty-seven

It took Emily a few days before she could bring herself to send a note to Lord Leventhorpe. He had called on her, but she had been out of the house on that particular afternoon. She did not dwell on what she and Frost had been doing that day while the earl sipped tea with her mother. Besides, what she had to say to the gentleman was not for her family's ears.

While she would have welcomed the privacy of his drawing room, she could not bring herself to enter his residence without a chaperone. Instead, Lord Leventhorpe had invited her to one of the tea gardens, and she had eagerly accepted the respectable setting.

"This concerns Lucy, does it not?" the earl asked once they were seated.

She lifted her brows in surprise. "I did not realize my intentions were so apparent."

"My dear, you have yet to learn how to conceal your emotions. The skill will be an invaluable asset if you choose to remain in town."

Lord Leventhorpe's mild lecturing tone had her

bristling with indignation, but she held her tongue. After this meeting, he would never have to speak to her again.

"My lord, you inquired after some of my sister's letters."

"Ah, yes . . . something to remind me of Lucy." Satisfaction gleamed in his gaze. "I assume your search was fruitful."

Instead of replying, Emily took a sip of her tea. "My sister has been dead more than five years, and I have learned more about her in the last few weeks than I did when she was still alive."

"You have been listening to old gossip. I would not put much faith in half-truths and lies."

Intrigued by his response, Emily tilted her head as she studied the man seated before her. "I assure you, my lord, I am aware that my sister was not the paragon my family believed her to be."

Lord Leventhorpe's mouth thinned in disapproval. "Who told you about her lover? Was it Chillingsworth?"

"No, it was someone else. How did you learn of it?"

"Lucy was not as clever as she thought about her indiscretions. At the time, obligations forced me to leave her unattended for months, and young ladies seek other amusements when they feel neglected. It was not long before people were whispering in my ear that Lucy's affections toward me had cooled."

"Did you confront her?"

"Naturally. I had every right. Your father and mother had been neglectful in their duties, and with a little persuasion Lucy confessed everything. The little fool had even convinced herself that her lover would marry her once he learned of the child she was carrying."

"You knew she was pregnant with another man's child," Emily said, feeling the world tilt beneath her feet again. "You must have been devastated by her betrayal."

Lord Leventhorpe slammed his fist against the table, causing her to flinch. "I was furious." He leaned closer. "I told your faithless sister that I wanted the bounder's name. She refused, knowing that I was prepared to put a bullet in his heart to appease my honor."

Emily had lost interest in her tea. "Is that what you did? Did you challenge her lover to a duel?"

"Unfortunately, my threats had little effect on the lady. She begged for my forgiveness, even offering to go through with the marriage to spare me the taint of scandal. Of course, I refused. I had no use for a duplicitous lady with a bastard in her belly."

The abrupt smile brightening his face was more chilling than his fury. "I have always wondered what Lucy had told you that final night. Your mother told me that you refused to speak of it, so I had assumed that she told you the truth."

"Does it bother you that I know?" she brazenly lied.

Lord Leventhorpe leaned forward, his expression revealing the malice he held in his heart. "Lucy deserved to be punished for her betrayal. I only took what she had given away for free."

Emily struggled to maintain her composure. "So you threatened her, abused her, and then tossed her out of your house."

"I did nothing any other man would not have done when faced with his lady's infidelity. The only decent thing Lucy did was to take her own life so the rest of us did not have to suffer through the scandal." He made a soft sound of annoyance. "My dear, don't look so shocked. Haven't you done everything possible to keep your sister's secrets?"

"Out of love." Emily cleared her throat. "I did it out of love."

"Then I am not the only one she made a fool of," he said, without an ounce of remorse that his violent confrontation had driven her sister to take her own life.

Emily had all the answers to the questions that had plagued her for years, and there was nothing she could do to change the outcome. There would be no justice for her sister.

She began to rise. "I should go."

"Wait." He seized her hand before she could stand. "What of the letters? Did you find them?"

"Why are these letters so important to you?"

"I never discovered the name of Lucy's lover." His fingers tightened over hers. "I know she wrote letters to him when they were separated. She had admitted as much. Then there were rumors that Chillingsworth and Lucy were lovers. I had caught her on several occasions flirting with the scoundrel, but I could never prove anything." When she did not react to his hurtful taunts, he pressed. "I want those letters, Emily."

She stood, tugging her hand free from his grasp. He would have drawn attention if he tried to reach for her again, so he resisted.

"It is the letters that I wished to discuss with you. I searched for them, and even went so far as to confront my mother about them. I was informed that my mother burned all personal correspondence out of respect for her daughter's privacy. In this, Lucy has bested you, Lord Leventhorpe. You will never learn the man's name."

Emily did not bother with farewells.

Now she understood why Lucy had whispered Frost's name. Out of fear for Captain Gladish, her sister must have hinted during her violent confrontation with the earl that Frost was her lover. Lord Chillingsworth was infamous for his skill on the dueling field, and Lord Leventhorpe would have been reluctant to challenge such an adversary. It was speculation on her part, but Lucy must have been worried that she had endangered an innocent gentleman with her lies. She had wanted Emily to warn Frost about Leventhorpe.

Distracted by her thoughts, she was not paying attention to where she was heading until she collided into someone. Emily looked up to apologize, but the words were caught in her throat as she locked gazes with Mr. Halward.

"Good afternoon, Miss Cavell," was his pleasant greeting. "You look rather upset. Perhaps I could be of service and see you home."

Emily edged away from him, but his fingers were clasped around her upper arm. "Thank you, Mr. Halward, but I would not wish to impose."

"Oh, this time I must insist, Miss Cavell," he said,

his grip constricting around her like a band of iron. "My coach is at your disposal."

Emily moved to the farthest wall of the compartment as Mr. Halward sat beside her. He did not speak until the coach began to move.

"You disappoint me, Miss Cavell."

"You are not the first to comment on my failings, Mr. Halward," she said, deciding that Lord Leventhorpe had been right about one thing. Her expressive face gave too much away.

"When we first met, I thought you might be a valuable ally when I learned of your sister's suicide and your dislike for Nox and clubs of their ilk." He noted her surprise, and she silently cursed. "Yes, I sensed there might be a connection, but I was never given a chance to indulge my curiosity. Suddenly Chillingsworth was sniffing at your skirts, and there was nothing I could do but wait for the gentleman to lose interest in the chase."

Mr. Halward gave her a pitying glance.

"Chillingsworth caught you, did he not?" He accepted her blush as confirmation. "I doubt your family is aware of the deep play you have been engaging in with the earl. Your father, in particular, would be quite distressed if he learned his daughter had been seduced. If I were him, I would worry that history was repeating itself."

"Your assumptions are rude, and none of your business," was her frigid response. "And I would refrain from spreading rumors about Lord Chillingsworth. Even you must be aware of his reputation on the dueling field. I doubt he would feel a twinge of regret if he had to put you down like a filthy animal."

"Oh, I have no doubt that Chillingsworth is already making plans to come after me." Mr. Halward chuckled. "That's where you might be a useful ally, after all."

"I do not understand."

"Perhaps you don't. Men rarely confide their violent thoughts to their lovers, and you are the earl's mistress, are you not?"

"I am friends with his sister. Nothing more."

"And I would like to believe you."

Emily cringed when he reached out and patted her on the knee.

He smiled genially at her. "But I don't."

"You know the police frown on kidnapping," she said, unable to keep the fear from her voice.

She assumed her father and Frost would disapprove, too.

"Kidnapping? Why, Miss Cavell, you have misunderstood my intentions."

Somehow Emily doubted it. "Then why am I here? I highly doubt you have offered to take me home out of the goodness of your heart."

"Your lack of faith in my sincerity wounds me to the quick. However, I am taking you home, Miss Cavell. Our little chat is merely to demonstrate that even skilled marksmen have vulnerabilities." His fingers dug into the soft flesh above her knee. "Chillingsworth needed a reminder, and you, my dear, will deliver my message."

The coach halted and Mr. Halward opened the

door. "You are home, Miss Cavell. I am counting on you to do your part."

Emily wondered if this was a trap, but was so relieved to escape the coach that she did not question her good fortune. She stepped over Mr. Halward's legs, and accepted the coachman's assistance as she disembarked.

She was not home.

Emily glanced over her shoulder, but the front door opened and Frost filled the doorway. He appeared as startled as she was to see her. Then his attention shifted to the coach behind her and his expression changed to pure loathing. She ignored Mr. Halward's low chuckle as she ran toward the man she loved.

Frost deftly caught her and hugged her so tightly that she cried out in pain. He whirled her around and carried her into his town house.

In his embrace, Emily did feel like she was home.

"I am going to murder the man."

Frost paced the floor of his library in front of Emily.

The shock of seeing her disembark from Halward's coach had him reaching for a decanter of brandy and two glasses. Frost managed to pour a good portion of brandy down her throat before she choked and begged him to stop. He finished her glass and poured a fresh one for himself.

If I lost Emily . . .

He banished the thought before he could finish it.

"Tell me again what he said to you," he demanded.

Emily repeated her brief exchange with the soon-to-be-very-dead Mr. Halward. The words *vulnerabilities* and *message* pealed like fucking bells in his head until he wanted to rage at her for the risks she took when she climbed into the coach with the bastard.

"It wasn't as if the man was giving me any choice," she muttered, and he realized that he had spoken out loud.

Frost's vision dimmed and he fought to hold on to the remaining shreds of his sanity. "And tell me why you were walking the streets of London without a servant at your heels?"

She deserved to be locked in her room for recklessness.

"Have you not been listening? I told you that I met Lord Leventhorpe at the tea garden," she said, sounding guarded.

"Why?"

Emily's eyes narrowed in suspicion, and he never credited her with lacking in intelligence or courage.

"It isn't important," she said, and he knew that she was lying. "Tell me that you aren't planning to challenge Halward. As you can see, I am unharmed. His mischief was meant to provoke you into rushing carelessly into what I can assume is some sort of trap." She frowned. "It was apparent the man does not like you."

"The feeling is mutual." Frost knelt down before her. "You are telling me the truth. The man didn't hurt you?"

"Mr. Halward rambled on about his disappointment in me and how he considered me an ally. He said that you needed a reminder of your vulnerabilities, but I wasn't sure of his meaning. Do you think he seeks to harm your sister and her family?"

"It is a possibility that I can't ignore," he said, clasping her hands and bowing his head.

He was not being entirely truthful. He understood Halward's message when he delivered her practically to his doorstep. Even if Emily was unaware of it, she was his vulnerability, and he could almost despise her for it.

"I will have one of my servants escort you home."

Emily grasped at him before he could pull away. "No, I want to stay with you. Please."

He stared down at her, regretting what he was about to do. "There is a reason why I never bring any of my lovers here. Mistresses come and go, but this is my home. It would become tiresome if I had to move every time I switched mistresses."

His words caught her by surprise but she quickly recovered. "Don't do this. You're not playing fair."

"Christ, Emily." He disengaged himself from her grasp and ran his hand through his hair. "When have I ever given you the impression that I play fair? In love or war, I always play to win."

Frost turned away so he did not have to look at the pain in her eyes.

"This isn't the real you." She stood and crossed her arms in a soothing gesture. "You are attempting to chase me off because you want to hunt down Halward. Please, I beg of you. Don't do it."

"Oh, Emily, wasn't Maryann proof enough that when I have finished with a lover, no amount of begging or tears can sway me." He shut his eyes. "We're done. Don't humiliate yourself in this fashion. I don't want you to end up like your sister. You're smarter than that."

She flinched as if he had slapped her. Her mouth trembled as she brought her fingers to her lips. "If you hope to make me despise you—congratulations, you've succeeded!"

Emily did not bother hiding her tears as she marched by him and into the front hall. He had already ordered the servants to watch over her. If she was angry enough to leave the house, one of them would follow her and make sure that she was safely returned to her family.

He walked over to the wall and rang for his butler.

Halward was expecting him, and Frost had no intention of disappointing him.

Chapter Twenty-eight

The butler had pleaded with her to wait as a carriage was readied for her, but Emily refused to remain a minute longer in the town house after she had been callously discarded by Lord Chillingsworth as if their time together had meant little to him. In the spirit of compromise, Sparrow had ordered one of the footmen to secure a hackney coach on her behalf.

Emily was not particular about her means of escape as long as the servants were quick about their task. Fortunately, the butler had some experience in dealing with highly emotional females, which did not surprise her in the slightest. Within minutes she was seated within the hired coach. She wondered if Frost was observing her departure from one of the windows. Highly doubtful, she thought, since he had been so determined to get rid of her.

When she had thanked Sparrow, the butler acknowledged her gratitude with a formal bow. As he closed the door of the hackney coach, he said, "It isn't my place, but I feel inclined to offer you some advice, Miss Cavell."

Good heavens! As if the afternoon could not get any worse. Emily had earned the man's pity. She tried to make light of her appalling predicament by offering the kind servant a wobbly smile. "It is kind of you, but I—"

"There are days when a man behaves badly for all the right reasons," Sparrow said cryptically.

"If you are trying to tell me that Lord Chillingsworth is an insufferable, condescending blackguard—then I concur," she said uncharitably, some of her former spirit returning. Frost might have bruised her feelings, but he was sorely mistaken if he believed she would allow him to have the last word on their friendship.

Unexpected delight crossed the butler's face. "Then you understand the earl better than most people, Miss Cavell. I look forward to chatting with you again."

Sparrow nodded to the coachman, and he turned away to return to the town house.

Emily opened her mouth to tell him that she had no reason to see him or Frost again, but saw no point in lying to the man. "Do you always offer parting advice to all of Lord Chillingsworth's former mistresses?"

The butler halted and glanced over his shoulder. "There has never been an occasion to do so, Miss Cavell. Such flighty creatures are not welcome in the earl's home. He only entertains family and close friends."

Sparrow continued toward the house.

The butler had already given the coachman directions to her family's town house. Emily leaned forward to rap on the small trapdoor to gain the man's attention.

"Aye, miss?" was his gruff reply.

"My plans have changed," Emily briskly explained. "Are you familiar with Lord and Lady Pashley's residence?"

It had been simple enough to deduce Halward's whereabouts with a few inquiries. After all, he wanted to be found. The man had nothing to fear since he believed that he held all the cards. He had plucked Emily off the streets, and was confident that he could do so again if his recent efforts had not enraged Frost sufficiently enough that he would willingly walk into what was obviously a trap. If Halward wanted a fight, Frost was in the mood to accommodate him.

Frost had hurt Emily. He was not proud of his ruthless tactics, but she would have tried to talk him out of confronting Halward, or worse, she would have warned his sister and Dare.

As if he needed anyone's help in dealing with the bastard.

For now, it was safer for Emily to remain angry with him. If she was preoccupied and furious with him, the last thing she would be contemplating was how to keep him away from Halward.

While it was a valiant effort, no self-respecting gent would consider yielding to a woman's demands when it came to protecting his interests. Even so, the anguish he had seen on Emily's face was tormenting him. Frost had longed to chase after her and beg for her forgiveness—and he would . . . eventually—once he and Halward had settled things between them.

Frost entered The Nag's Court, an old public house not far from Nox. The establishment had seen better days and patrons, but he was not one to judge another man's pleasures.

He nodded to the barkeeper and got down to business. "Where is Halward?"

The man was shorter, but Frost suspected that most of the bulk pressing on the seams of his clothing was muscle rather than fat. "Is he expecting ye?"

"Aye. Most definitely," he replied, idly wondering if he would have to fight his way out of the public house when he was finished with Halward. "And you know as well as I that he doesn't like to be kept waiting."

"Out back." The barkeeper caught the attention of a young lad who had been sweeping the floor. "The boy will show ye the way."

Frost followed the boy through a narrow gloomy passageway, the only light coming from the open door at the end. He stepped out into a small yard. It was as uninspiring as the interior of the public house, with a small stagnant pond that could have been mistaken for the devil's bunghole. A few scrawny hens pecked at the mud while two dogs fought as several spectators placed wagers on the outcome.

Halward glanced up and looked startled as Frost approached him and his guards, but he hastily concealed his genuine reaction. His gaze hardened as his hands parted in a welcoming gesture. "Chillingsworth, I was just telling my companions that it was very unlikely that you would be so foolish as to show up alone. Where are your friends?"

Before Frost had left his town house, he had had a similar conversation with his butler. Once Halward's whereabouts had been discovered, Sparrow had become quite distressed at the news that his employer had no intention of contacting the other Lords of Vice. Granted, Halward's unhealthy fascination in Nox and his attack on Berus concerned all of them, but the man had made it personal when he had abducted Emily.

Halward thought he was dealing with a spineless aristocrat who would crumble at his first taste of violence. The man had certainly provoked the wrong gent. Without a misstep in his stride, in one fluid motion his fist connected with Halward's nose. The bewilderment and pain widened the man's eyes as he staggered backward. Bright red blood flowed from his ruined nose. Arrogant and stupid. With his guards stationed beside him like silent mountains, he had assumed few men were daring enough to challenge him.

"What did you expect? Pistols at dawn?" Frost spat, leveling a vicious kick into the man's groin.

Halward shrieked and dropped to the ground.

Frost barely had time to take a breath before the two bruisers were on him. Later he might regret his strategy of striking Halward first, but the man's startled expression and the satisfying crunch of his nose breaking would be worth the pain.

The blond guard landed a respectable punch to Frost's ribs. Frost returned the favor by driving his clenched fingers into his attacker's throat. The blow was cushioned by the man's cravat, but he was more concerned about drawing his next breath than hitting Frost.

"Take him down!" Halward shouted over the barking dogs.

The dark-haired bastard tackled him and Frost landed facedown into the dirt. As he violently struggled to get free, the man landed several hits to Frost's right side. He grunted against the pain and blindly lashed out with his bent elbow. The first few swings met only air, but the third connected with the man's cheek. Frost rolled out of reach only to have his ankle captured by the blond.

Perhaps confronting Halward without the support of his friends had not been such a sound plan. If Frost did not gain the upper hand, he would end up castrated and his testicles would be fed to the half-starved dogs.

Like hell.

Frost kicked the blond as hard as he could. The man collapsed and remained down. He struggled to his feet, ready to fight the dark-headed mountain of muscle, and was dumbstruck to see Sin, Dare, and Hunter standing in the yard. Sin had his arm wrapped around his attacker's thick neck while Hunter had a pistol pointed at the man's chest. Dare had his pistol aimed in Halward's direction.

"Took all of you long enough," Frost said, fighting to keep his voice level. He had not asked for their help, but his friends had been there for him anyway. "Where are the others?"

"Keeping the barkeeper and the few remaining

patrons company," Dare said, not taking his gaze off Halward. "We were not certain who was loyal to your friends here."

"They are no friends of mine, gent," Frost replied, brushing the dirt from his frock coat and trousers. He walked over to Halward and crouched down.

With a bloodied handkerchief pressed against his nose, the man silently glared at him.

"The next time you fancy taking over a club, you might try stealing one of the bastions of respectability at the top of St. James's Street. Nox is off limits to you and your friends."

Frost slowly straightened. "Oh, just one more thing. This is for abducting Miss Cavell."

The punch clipped the man on the underside of his chin. Halward's head snapped back, and he dropped like a stone. Rubbing the sting out of his bruised knuckles, Frost was content to leave Halward and his people's fate to the magistrate.

He groaned as an unpleasant thought occurred to him.

"What's wrong?" his brother-in-law asked. "Are you hurt?"

"No, I just realized that I will have to sack Sparrow for defying my orders," Frost said, believing his butler was responsible for his friends' timely arrival. "Damn . . . I hate this because I genuinely like the man."

"Sparrow wasn't the one who told us your plans," Sin said, tightening his hold on the dark-haired guard and causing him to grimace. "It was Emily."

Chapter Twenty-nine

A few days later, behind closed doors, Frost, Sin, Reign, Saint, Hunter, Vane, and Dare sat down once again to discuss the fate of their club. Nox had been a part of their lives so long, and the gaming hell was profitable.

"I don't want to shut the doors."

Sin rubbed his forehead as if anticipating the headache he would develop from what would likely be a lively debate.

"Neither do I, Frost," Sin said, dropping his hand as he met his gaze. "You seem surprised. I don't believe there is a single person here who wants to let the club go."

"Halward is not the first man to cause problems for Nox," Vane interjected.

Dare nodded. "Nor will he be the last."

Reign braced his forearms on the wooden table. "I never thought I would be saying this, but it is a matter of priorities. Our lives have changed. Just because I would rather spend my evenings with Sophia and Lily Grace doesn't mean any of you are less important to me. I am willing to help you manage Nox, but no longer wish to spend my entire life here."

The simmering anger he usually felt when one of his friends spoke of shifting responsibilities had cooled to acceptance. Frost finally understood that his friends had not turned their backs on their friendships or Nox. When he had been fighting for his life, his friends had been there for him. The wild days of drinking and whoring till dawn had vanished, and none of them mourned the loss. They had filled the emptiness in their lives by marrying good women and starting their families.

Saint smirked. "I have a feeling our wives might have a thing or two to say about us entertaining prostitutes in the private saloon."

Sin laughed. "I'll say. Though Madame Venna's girls did brighten up the private rooms."

Hunter got right down to the unspoken question. "Do we stay or sell, gents?"

All of them looked at Frost. As the remaining bachelor, they were letting him make the decision. They would honor whatever he decided. Frost stood and flattened his palms on the table.

"Nox stays open."

No one appeared surprised by his decision. He appreciated that no one groaned, either. "I have a few conditions."

Vane rolled his eyes, but Frost ignored him.

"What kind of changes," Sin asked.

"New members. All of you have been shortening

your time here, and Nox needs new blood if it's to remain open and profitable."

Reign appeared intrigued. "Are you suggesting that we hand all of our hard work to someone else?"

"Not at all," Frost said. "We are founding members; all rights and privileges remain in place. The new members can run the club. Berus can look after them."

The steward's expression brightened as he realized that the Lords of Vice were not shutting down Nox. "Thank you for your confidence, Lord Chillingsworth."

"I assume you have some gentlemen in mind?"

Frost glanced at Dare. "Aye, a few. The Earl of Ashenhurst and his twin brother . . . Lord Macestone and Lord Wilderspin—"

Vane snorted and whispered something to Saint, who nodded.

Frost gave them a knowing grin. "Ashenhurst and his friends will likely be barbed thorns in our collective arses. And I give you full permission to remind me that I nominated them when I try to murder them. By the by, Ashenhurst's father approached me a few days ago. The duke was impressed that I had managed to make a suitable impression on his unruly sons and he has asked me to continue to do so."

Saint did not look convinced. "So we make them Lords of Vice?"

"They already are, according to their sire," Frost drily replied. "He figures it will take all of us to pound some sense into them."

"It could be fun," Reign said, grinning at the prospect of tormenting their new members. "We could view it as practice for when Sin's and Dare's sons are older."

The notion had Sin dropping his face into his hands. "Christ!"

All of them laughed.

"Anyone else?" Vane asked.

"I look forward to your suggestions, but I recommend one more gentleman." Frost hesitated because he knew he would have some opposition. "Lord Ravens."

Sin lifted his head. "No. The man is more arrogant than you."

"I agree. He is tolerable company," Saint said, recalling the nights he and Frost had spent at the earl's town house.

"Are you certain, Frost?" Hunter said, leaning forward. "I know he is your friend, but Ravens and the Lords of Vice have never gotten along. It was one of the reasons why we rejected nominating him seven years ago."

"I am not fond of the man," Vane grumbled.

"We need more than puppies in Nox, Vane," Frost argued. "Ravens will help Berus watch over Nox when we aren't around."

"And what about you, Frost," Dare softly queried. "What will you be doing while Ravens is corrupting our new members?"

With a wolfish grin on his handsome face, Frost said, "Learning how to shift my priorities, gents."

* * *

Emily stepped into the front hall, nodding to the groom whose arms were laden with her purchases. "Good afternoon, Martha. Is my mother upstairs?"

"Yes, Miss Cavell." She began to relieve the groom of his burden. "She has a guest in the drawing room."

Emily untied her bonnet and removed her gloves. Martha had enough to handle, so she placed her accessories on the rectangular table. "Don't worry about them. I'll collect them after I speak to my mother."

She grasped her skirt and made her way up the staircase. Her afternoon outing with the wives of the Lords of Vice had been enjoyable and informative. Because she was Regan's friend, she had been warmly welcomed into their group. When they had parted, she had felt that they were slowly becoming her friends, too.

"Mother, I have just returned from—" Emily swallowed the rest of her words at the sight of Frost sitting beside her mother on the sofa.

He stood the second she stepped into the drawing room.

"Did you have a nice outing, my dear?" her mother inquired.

Emily stared at Frost. His presence was unexpected and a delight. "Yes. Later, I will show you what I've purchased." To Frost, she asked, "What are you doing here? Regan said that all the Lords of Vice were meeting at Nox to discuss the club's future."

"For once, the seven of us managed to agree on what's right for Nox." He moistened his lips. "You look beautiful."

There was something in his inflection that nudged her mother to glance up. Her gaze shifted from Frost to her daughter. Neither one of them was paying any attention to her.

"You know, I don't think I can wait," she said, walking toward Emily. "I might as well take a quick peek at your purchases. Did Martha put them in your bedchamber?"

"Yes, Mother." Appreciating that she was giving them a private moment to speak, Emily smiled at her mother as she passed by her. "Thank you."

"Of course." Her mother paused at the door. "Look after my girl, Lord Chillingsworth."

"Yes, madam," he formally replied, moving to Emily's side when her mother shut the door. "I have a few matters to address with you, Miss Cavell."

"But first things first." Frost pulled her into his arms and kissed her. The nerves jangling in his stomach eased when she kissed him back with a need that bordered on desperation.

"I have missed you," Emily whispered.

"Good," he said, her eyes opening at his arrogance. "A man wants his woman to appreciate him. The next time you are vexed with me, you might be quicker to forgive me."

Emily laid her cheek against his chest, and then abruptly drew back. "His woman?"

"Aye, his . . . or mine." With his hands resting

lightly on her hips, he lowered his head until it touched hers. "I wasn't sure you would ever speak to me again. Not that I don't deserve it. I owe you an apology."

Emily shook her head as she pulled away. "A clever woman would have you on your knees while you make that apology, but I knew what you were about, Lord Chillingsworth, even if I did not like it. I was upset and you—"

Frost gave her a little shake. "None of that. You were hurt and angry, and justifiably so. You have every reason to make me suffer. I was an arse, but you were—right."

She blinked at him. He felt as if he had swallowed a frog whole, but a man's pride was rarely palatable.

"I was wrong, too," she admitted. "You kept telling me to look beyond your notorious reputation and truly see you as a man, flaws and all. In my defense, I was blinded by fear. I misunderstood what Lucy had been trying to tell me, when she whispered your name." She glanced away. "I was also afraid of my feelings for you."

His turquoise-blue gaze warmed with affection. "And exactly how do you feel about me, Emily Cavell?" He tugged her closer and nipped her lower lip. "Is it possible that you fell in love with me, hmm? Maybe just a little?"

"If I say *yes*, does that make me a silly little girl who doesn't know the difference between lust and love?" she asked, her hazel eyes brimming with unshed tears.

He did not want to make her cry.

"No, Em," he said, cradling her face in his hands. "It makes me the luckiest gent in all of England."

He lowered his head and kissed her, his mouth reverently moving against hers. A ragged sob escaped as she wrapped her arms around his neck and held him.

"I love you, Frost!"

He closed his eyes. Sagging against her, bowing his head until his chin rested on the top of her head. "It's a good thing, too. About an hour ago, I spoke to your father. I told him that you needed a keeper, and he agreed. He has given us his blessing to marry."

"Marriage."

He frowned, slightly offended that she had not considered the possibility. "Have you not been paying attention? I intend to marry you."

Emily brought her hand to her mouth, then turned away from him as she struggled not to cry.

Frost felt guilty, and belatedly it occurred to him that she might not wish to marry him at all. "Em, have I been such a bounder that you didn't think I would marry you?"

Through her tears, he had managed to make her laugh. "Your life has been Nox, gambling, and mistresses. You have made it clear to all and sundry that you proposed to remain forever unfettered. Marriage was never in your plans."

Frost took her by the hand and led her to the sofa. When he sat down, he pulled her onto his lap so he had an excuse to cuddle her. She trembled, and he sensed that she was fighting not to break down.

"You're right, I assumed I would never marry. Why should I? I believed I had everything I wanted in life." He tenderly wiped away a tear from her cheek. "Then I met you. Beautiful, wary, unimpressed with my charms . . . the one woman I longed to have, and for a long time she thought I might have seduced and abandoned her sister."

"I never wanted to believe that you had hurt Lucy," she protested. "Nor were my concerns much of an obstacle. You still managed to seduce me."

"I was a desperate man, Em." He stroked her hair. "I thought one taste of your innocence would sustain me, but I only hungered for more, even while I fought you and myself." He shook his head. "I wasn't supposed to fall in love."

She tried to smile. "You love me."

He entwined his hand with hers and kissed her knuckles. "So much so, the depths of my feelings frightened me. With the exception of my sister, no woman has ever held the power to destroy me until you."

"I would never hurt you," she protested, visibly appalled at the notion.

"I know. However, it wasn't just you. It was this business with Halward, Nox, and the unspoken sense of loss I was feeling as my friends abandoned me, one by one."

"Frost, your friends haven't abandoned you."

"I know. It just took me longer to figure it out." Frost brushed a kiss against her lips.

"Em, does Mother know that Lord Chillingsworth

is fondling you in the drawing room?" Cedric asked, standing in the doorway.

"Oh, do go away, Cedric," Emily said, gazing into Frost's eyes.

"Heed your sister, puppy," Frost said, smiling at her. "Now run along."

Cedric stomped out the room. "Mother," he shouted. "Do you know what Emily is doing with—"

"Cedric, be a good boy and leave your sister alone. Lord Chillingsworth is in the middle of proposing to our Emily." Her mother's voice could be heard from the landing above.

"Welcome to the family," Cedric muttered, not sounding pleased at all. He stalked off.

"Now you have to marry me, if only to annoy your brother," Frost teased. "But you have yet to give me a proper answer."

"Your friends and your club are important to you," she said, looking much too serious for a lady who had just received a sincere proposal of marriage. "I would not ask you to give your old life up. However, it makes little sense to marry, when Nox and the problems that come with it will always come first with you."

"If you believe that then you are not listening," Frost countered. "My friends adore you almost as much as I do, and it is obvious their wives consider you part of the family. As for Nox, it represents a large, maddening, and wonderful part of my life, and I will always have a connection to it. That is not to say that changes aren't in order. I've spoken to my friends, and we've decided to take on new members. The club needs fresh blood, and Berus and Lord Ravens can oversee it—though I have yet to share the good news with the gent. This will allow me to concentrate on more important things."

Something akin to hope lit up her face. "Like what?"

He playfully tapped her on the nose. "You. I have prided myself in not playing by the rules, but no more. I want you to understand how much you mean to me, and I will do anything and everything to properly bind you to me. No special licenses or dashing off to Gretna Green. I want the banns posted, seamstresses summoned to create a special dress for your wedding, and my house prepared for a bride. I want to stand before my family, friends, and the entire bloody *ton* so no one will ever doubt my commitment to you."

"Frost, it is a lofty promise. Not that I doubt your sincerity. However, no one changes their nature at whim."

"You're right."

Emily tried to climb out of his lap, but he hooked her around the waist and pulled her back where she belonged.

"You consider me as a wild, reckless fellow who will never give up his ways."

"I never said—"

Frost placed a finger on her lips. "Hush. Well then . . . there is only one thing to do." She laughed as he tipped her back until she was lying on the sofa cushions.

He climbed on to top of her, bracing his arms near her head. "I won't give up my nature."

Emily's face fell at his declaration.

"But I am willing to compromise. What if I was only wild and reckless with you?"

Emily's lips twitched as she tried not to laugh. "It's a very tempting offer. I would be mad to refuse."

"Then I am glad we are in agreement." He stood and held out his hand. "Now come along."

"Where are we going?"

"Our house. I want you naked in my bed. I want to slip away before your mother decides to invite me for supper."

When Emily didn't move, he bent down and tossed her over his shoulder.

"Frost!"

"There's no time to argue, love. I assure you, once your father learns your whereabouts, he will feel honor-bound to collect you."

"My father will not be pleased with either of us if he finds me in bed with the most infamous Lord of Vice of all."

"Don't fret. I intend to ruin you most thoroughly. When I am finished, he will let me keep you."

"Your arrogance is astounding," she muttered as he carried her down the stairs.

"As are my skills as a lover," he boasted, confident that his soon-to-be bride would agree.

It wasn't until they reached the bottom of the staircase that Frost allowed her feet to touch the ground.

He kissed her on the nose. "For the rest of the evening I will be happy to demonstrate that some vices are worth the surrender."

"Ah, my favorite lesson," Emily said, her hazel eyes shining up at him with love, joy, and laughter. "Lead on, my beloved scoundrel."

Don't miss these other Lords of Vice novels by
USA Today bestselling author

ALEXANDRA HAWKINS

"Sizzling, smart, and sophisticated."
—Gaelen Foley, *New York Times* bestselling author

DUSK WITH A DANGEROUS DUKE

ALL AFTERNOON WITH
A SCANDALOUS MARQUESS

SUNRISE WITH A NOTORIOUS LORD

AFTER DARK WITH A SCOUNDREL

TILL DAWN WITH THE DEVIL

ALL NIGHT WITH A ROGUE

Available from St. Martin's Paperbacks